The Search

The Search

A Novel

GEOFF DYER

Graywolf Press

First published in Great Britain in 1993 by Hamish Hamilton

This publication is made possible, in part, by the voters of Minnesota through a
Minnesota State Arts Board Operating Support grant, thanks to a legislative ap-
propriation from the arts and cultural heritage fund, and through grants from the
National Endowment for the Arts and the Wells Fargo Foundation Minnesota.
Significant support has also been provided by Target, the McKnight Foundation,
Amazon.com, and other generous contributions from foundations, corporations, and
individuals. To these organizations and individuals we offer our heartfelt thanks.

Published by Graywolf Press
250 Third Avenue North, Suite 600
Minneapolis, Minnesota 55401

www.graywolfpress.org

Published in the United States of America

ISBN 978-1-55597-678-1

2 4 6 8 9 7 5 3 1
First Graywolf Printing, 2014

Library of Congress Control Number: 2013958010

Cover design: Dan McKinley

Cover art: Keith Negley

for Fi

Fairy-tales and legends often tell of a knight who suddenly catches sight of a rare bird of which he then sets off in pursuit, since in the beginning it seemed quite close, but then it flies off again, until at last night falls. The knight is separated from his companions and lost in the wilderness in which he now finds himself. SØREN KIERKEGAARD

The man who has criss-crossed every ocean has merely criss-crossed the monotony of his self. I have criss-crossed more seas than any man alive. I have seen more mountains than most on this earth. I have been through more cities than exist and over the mighty rivers of non-existent worlds which flowed, absolute, under my contemplative gaze . . .

Did I leave? I could not swear to it. I found myself in other lands, in other ports, passing through towns which were not this one, even if neither this one nor that one were towns at all . . . FERNANDO PESSOA

THE SEARCH BEGAN WHEN WALKER MET RACHEL.

He had been hung-over most of the day and intended taking it easy that night. Then, just as he was beginning to feel better, his brother dropped by, kitted out in an off-white tuxedo, telling Walker to get changed and get a move on, he was coming to Charles and Margot Browning's party.

'I haven't got a tux.'

'There's one in the car. Come on, we're late. Let's go.'

They were annual events, these parties, renowned throughout the Bay for the extravagant array of drink and food, the wealth of those invited to consume it. Walker had never been before and apart from his brother—who, it emerged in the car, had come by the invite indirectly—he knew no one. He stood drinking, squeezed into a wine-stained tuxedo, wondering why he had come. Photographers were prowling around, snapping anyone who possessed the distinctive complexion of wealth. No one had any interest in photographing Walker but several times he was caught in the blurred background of a smiling society couple.

He had been there an hour, getting loaded, watching people talk, when a woman nudged into him and spilt half his drink. His

1

age, a little older maybe. Brown hair piled up, earrings, no lipstick.
A dress that reached to the floor.

'Oh, I'm sorry.'

Walker dabbed at his jacket.

'That's OK.'

She was laughing. 'It looks a little on the tight side.'

'That's how they're being worn this year.'

'A dinner jacket and surgical truss in one. Very stylish.'

'I like to think so.'

She said her name, reached out a bare arm. Her bracelets
chimed together as he shook her hand.

'It's a terrible party, isn't it?'

In the first moments of meeting someone we're attracted to
we grope towards an agreement on something, however small—
even if it is only agreeing to have a drink—and this declaration
of Rachel's was enough to establish a treaty between them. They
bitched about the party, the people there. Watched one of the
photographers coax a grin and kiss from a pair of rival celebrities.

'It's funny,' she said. 'Nothing means anything any more unless you're photographed doing it. We need photos to prove to
everyone else we exist, to remind ourselves. How's that for an un-
original thought? What were we talking about? I forget.'

'Photos,' said Walker. 'Pictures.'

'Yes. You know when you're on holiday and you take pictures?
You always wait until you're back home before getting them de-
veloped, even if you have time. Otherwise they're just postcards.
But if you wait till you're back home they're different. Then it's
like that story of dreaming of a garden where you pick a flower—
and you wake up with petals in your bed.'

She was high or drunk, Walker guessed. 'I never take a camera,' he said dully.

'So the dream goes on, even after you've woken up. Either that or you don't wake up at all.' She took a sip of red wine, holding the glass in both hands—a gesture Walker had always been a sucker for.

'Something like that,' he said. Seeing his glass was empty, Rachel motioned to him to take hers. As she did so a photographer crouched down and snapped them. Walker took a gulp of Rachel's wine. A guy in a red-faced blazer came over and kissed her, chatted and drifted away, leaving them alone again. Moments later a woman came up and kissed Rachel on the cheek, introduced her to a man with a millionaire haircut who in turn presented another man to her. Suddenly there was a lot of kissing going on. Eventually Walker got included in the swelling round of introductions. Shook hands, repeated his name for those who didn't quite catch it. He finished Rachel's wine, mumbled 'Excuse me' to no one in particular and headed for the bar.

Rachel was surrounded by a laughing group of people when he got back. He handed her a full glass and she smiled thanks. The way she laughed, looked at him. Walker wondered if he would go to bed with her, not now, not tonight, sometime. The possibility hovered beyond the edge of what they said which was nothing, just words and smiles swapped. He shuffled on the periphery of the group and moved off, bumping into someone as he did so.

'Sorry!' It was the kind of party where people were constantly stepping into each other and apologizing. On this occasion, though, the guy Walker had collided with stood there and stared him down as if they were in a waterfront bar where an encounter like this could lead to a broken-bottle fight. A camera flashed whitely behind the guy's head, silhouetting him briefly. Now he was looking over Walker's shoulder; Walker glanced around, instinctively following his gaze, thought he glimpsed Rachel looking away, startled.

Walker moved off, shoving gently through the crowd. Lifted a bottle from a waiter's tray and resumed his solitary drinking. He was out on the terrace, looking down at the glinting waters of the bay, when he felt a touch on his arm. He turned round and saw her.

'I thought I'd never find you,' she said. 'It's so crowded.'

'I'm glad you did.'

'I'm sorry, I got cornered. Is there anything more boring than a party?'

'Hundreds of things—but at a party it's more concentrated. And it happens on a bigger scale.'

She smiled quickly, 'I have to leave. I wanted to say good-bye.'

'That's a shame.'

'Yes. I would like to have talked to you more.'

'Maybe I'll call you.'

'It's better if I call you.'

'Yes?'

'Are you in the book?'

'Yes. It's under B: B for Brush-off.'

'I'm not giving you the brush-off—it's a weird expression, isn't it? Honestly.'

'OK.'

'I'll call you.'

With that she was gone, leaving Walker in the mothy darkness, an empty bottle in his hand.

Two days later she turned up at his apartment. A fresh, clear morning. He had just got back from the gym and was sitting on the patio, reading the paper, when the doorbell rang. The mailman, he guessed.

She was wearing jeans, a sweatshirt. Her hair, neatly pinned up at the party, was all over the place today. In her hand she held a pile of letters.

'Your mail,' she smiled.

Walker looked over her shoulder and waved at the retreating figure of the mailman, smiling and pleased now that the good weather was here.

Walker smiled too. Everyone was smiling. 'Come in.'

'Is this a bad time?'

'It's a perfect time.'

Walker fixed a jug of orange and she followed him out to the patio. They sat in creaking wicker chairs, filling pauses with the swirl and chink of ice. He tore open one of the letters she had handed him and glanced at the contents. Sunlight bounced white off the painted concrete. Walker squinted while she put on a pair of sunglasses. At every moment her face seemed on the brink of answering 'No' to the question 'Is she beautiful?' But the answer never quite came and the longer he looked the more uncertain he became. Later, he saw he had got it wrong all the time: her beauty lay precisely in this aura of uncertainty. Beside it the beauty of models and actresses seemed banal. At the time, watching her finger a strand of hair from her face, he was aware only of the way his eyes lingered on her as they waited for each other to speak.

'I think you said the other night that you're not working just now,' she said at last.

'That's right.'

'So what do you do all day?'

'You know, the time passes.'

'Pleasantly?'

'It passes.'

'What did you do before this?'

5

'Various things. Drifted from one thing to another. Whatever came up.'

'You've never had a job?'

'Off and on. Off mainly.'

'And what do you do for money?'

'Are you a social worker?'

'I'm just interested.'

'Odds and ends. My brother's renovating a house just north of the bay. I work for him now and again. Maybe you met him the other night?'

She shook her head, took a sip of orange. The imprint of her lip appeared on the cold glass, fading as he noticed it.

'You're being too modest. I think you've had a more interesting life than you let on.'

'Oh?'

'Yes. I think you've been involved in quite a few interesting things. Not all of them quite legal.'

'If you say so.'

'You're trying very hard to be enigmatic, Mr Walker.'

'I know, I'm putting everything into it.'

'Perhaps it would be a help if you borrowed these,' she said, handing him her sunglasses.

'That's much better,' Walker said when he had put them on.

'They suit you.'

'Thank you.'

'How was prison?'

'It was great. Bit cloudy a couple of days but the rest of the time it was terrific,' he said and chucked the remains of his drink at her. 'Now fuck off out of my house.'

She brushed the melting ice from her lap, surprised but unruffled.

'Dramatic,' she said, only the faintest hint of nervousness in her voice. Seeing him smile she went on, 'Do you really want me to leave?'

Walker was watching her carefully from behind the sunglasses. Her knees parted, almost imperceptibly, a quarter of an inch, no more, as she spoke. With his empty glass he gestured for her to continue.

'For a while you worked as a tracker.'

'Not exactly.'

'You found Orlando Brandon.'

'I came across him. By accident.'

'A very fortunate accident. For you, at any rate. People had been looking for him for three years. The buy-out must have been considerable.'

Walker waited, studying her.

'Not so fortunate for him, however,' she said. 'If I remember rightly, he was dead three weeks after you found him.'

'Four.'

She dug around in her bag and found another pair of sunglasses. Blew dust off the lenses.

'How many pairs do you have in there?'

'This is the last,' she said, her eyes disappearing behind the shades. 'I would like you to find someone for me.'

'That's illegal. Besides, like I told you, I was never a tracker.'

'I appreciate that, Mr Walker, but I will, if I may, explain myself a little further.'

Walker shrugged. 'What's all this Mr Walker bit?'

'The situation seems to demand it,' she smiled. 'Can I continue?'

Walker nodded. Shrugs, nods, smiles.

'Have you heard of Alexander Malory?'

'No. Should I have done?'

'There have been a number of articles in the paper about him.'

'I don't read the papers.'

'Well, he's disappeared.'

'A lot of people disappear. Or try to.'

'Hence the need for trackers.'

'What's your interest in him?'

'I am his wife.' On cue she removed her sunglasses. As an expression of frankness it was so perfectly executed that Walker suspected it might not be genuine. 'We're separated. That was years ago. He was very generous. Since then, however, certain irregularities in his dealings have come up. The police are interested in him. They don't yet have a warrant for him but they will have one soon. There are other people interested in him also. To speak plainly, they want to kill him. It's possible he is trying to evade them but he moves around a lot anyway. It's equally possible he is just off travelling. Earlier I said he had disappeared—in a way he is in a state of constant disappearance.'

'And?'

'And I want to find him. For two reasons. If he is simply travelling, I would like to warn him—as I say, our parting was entirely amicable.' Walker poured more orange into her glass. 'The second reason applies wherever or whatever he's doing. My lawyers have found a loophole in our arrangements. I need him to sign and fingerprint a copy of one of our contracts.'

'Fingerprint?'

'It's a new legal requirement with certain documents. I don't know why. But once he's done that, whatever happens to him, everything comes to me. He has to sign this before the police get to him. If he dies or is arrested before this document is signed, I lose everything.'

'Everything you have or everything you have coming to you?'

'Both.'

Walker had been studying her closely. Now, suddenly aware that she was scrutinizing him, he asked hurriedly, 'So why me? There are trackers who—'

'Too unreliable. It's quite possible that trackers have already been employed to find him—by the people who want to kill him.'

'But why me?'

'As I said, you've had a more interesting life than you let on. You could do it. You're not doing anything else. And you're restless.'

'How do you know I'm restless?'

'I meant you're totally content. Is that better?'

'Yes, it doesn't matter,' Walker said, smiling.

'I have no idea what it will involve,' Rachel continued. 'It's possible you will find him in a few days. It is equally possible that he has genuinely disappeared and has camouflaged his tracks— in which case finding him will be more difficult. Either way the important thing is that you find him before anyone else.'

'So you want me to find him and get him to sign and finger-print a piece of paper. That's all?'

'Yes.'

'And what if he doesn't want to sign this new will or contract or whatever?'

'Then perhaps you mention that there are people who wish to see him dead and who would pay a lot to know his where-abouts. It won't come to that. Like I said, Alex has always been generous to me.'

'And—' Walker paused '—why is this of interest to me?'

'First, I will pay you a great deal of money. Tell me, how much did you make from finding Orlando Brandon?'

'Enough.'

'Whatever you earned for finding Brandon, I will pay double. More than enough, you might say.'

Walker raised his eyebrows as if to say, 'That's a very generous offer.'

'I think it is not the money that will interest you. It is the case itself. You will have very little to go on. It will be a challenge. For example, Alex hated—hates—being photographed. There is no photograph of him as far as I can discover.'

'Not even a passport?'

'He has that with him.'

'And are trackers already after him?'

'Impossible to tell.'

'How long since you heard from him?'

'Six months.'

Walker was tugging at his right earlobe with thumb and forefinger. She pointed at his ear and said, 'You'll end up with one ear longer than the other.'

'What?'

'Pulling your ear like that.'

'My father used to do it. It's a gesture I've inherited.'

Their glasses were empty apart from melting ice.

'Well?'

'I'll call you,' he said, and this time she gave him her number.

The strangeness of her story bothered Walker less than the way it challenged his gathering sense of inertia. He had been drifting for months, uncertain what to do, forming vague plans but lacking the resolution to see anything through. He was waiting for a decisive moment—a moment that would impel him to make a decision—but no such moment came. Every morning he had breakfast at the Café Madrid and walked down to the ocean. Every other day he lifted weights. Afternoons he went running along the beach. Evenings he drank. His growing addiction to this regime of fitness—and the drinking it served to offset—was one of a number of small details that made him postpone any commitment to change. He had so little to do that even minor chores like going to the bank became major events in his day. The more he pondered things the more restless he became, floundering in a sea of impulses. He had no responsibilities, no obligations, and so found himself paralysed by choice, waiting to see what came his way. Now something had come his way—a challenge, she had said—and he balked at the prospect, longed instead for his current life to continue indefinitely and without interruption.

Tracking: he turned the word over in his mind, taking the measure of his feelings. After Brandon's death he'd sworn—not sworn, to swear not to do something always seemed like an incitement to do it—he'd resolved not to get involved in anything like that again, especially now, now that it was illegal, dangerous.

Six years previously tracking had been an industry virtually. It started as a response to rewards being offered for information regarding the whereabouts of prominent figures who had gone missing. One case attracted a lot of publicity when the man claiming the reward called himself a professional tracker. The term caught on and the numbers of people disappearing, it seemed to Walker, increased in order to keep pace with the growing numbers of people calling themselves trackers. It got to the point where, like lights left on in an empty house, a pile of clothes left on a beach was taken as a sign not of accidental drowning but of an inadequate attempt to disguise a disappearance. Whenever anyone disappeared there was always somebody who had a vested interest in finding him or her again. Anyone with a taste for adventure was lured into the idea of tracking; the classified pages of small-town papers always included a few ads from trackers offering their services. Even the government department responsible for missing persons—Finders to themselves and everyone else—was getting in on the act. A number of officers were alleged to have located a missing person and then sold the information to a private concern. Finders keepers, it was commonly joked, was the motto of the Missing Persons' Department. Lured by the prospect of big money, anyone in the department with ambition and initiative went solo after a few years. The government moved quickly: missing persons, it ruled, had to be investigated by the government department only. Tracking was illegal without a licence—and a licence became impossible to obtain. The move backfired: putting trackers beyond the law meant that a lot of people living outside the law got in on tracking. Many trackers had been less than reliable or scrupulous in their methods, but now that they were firmly outside the law their methods became increasingly ruthless. Like trafficking, tracking became one of the standard activities of the underworld. And this was the world Walker was being lured back into.

The day after Rachel's visit he walked along the beach, hearing the freeway roar of the ocean, feeling the fling and reach of spray. He picked a curve of brown glass from the sand. Sea lions were clowning in the breaking waves. A dog scampered after a chewed husk of ball. Clumps of kelp, driftwood.

Later, when the light was turning hazy, he called her from a telephone on the boardwalk. He had not known what he was going to say when he dialled her number but hearing her voice he decided on impulse. Yes, he said, he'd do it.

They spent a day together, sitting outside in the first warm sun of the year. Rachel was wearing a pale dress and a cardigan, one button missing. Walker asked her to tell him everything about Malory, the people he knew, his business contacts, his habits. Whenever he asked for more details she paused and answered his questions patiently. Walker made notes, so intent on watching her speak that at times he did not hear what she was saying. He drifted, thinking of the happiness that might lie in wait for them. Then he was jolted back to the present. Rachel was telling him of the allegations of corruption that had come in the wake of Malory's winning a huge bridge-building contract.

'You didn't hear about it?'

'No. Sorry. Like I said, I never read papers.'

'Television?'

'Only sport.'

'Not films even?'

'Not really.'

'Alex—'

'If I find him,' Walker interrupted, 'you just want me to get those documents signed?'

'Yes.'

'You don't want me to bring him back?'

'I think you're not being quite honest again, Mr Walker.'

'What do you mean?'

'I think you do watch films. Old ones. And no, all I want are the documents.'

'Did he have affairs?'

'I don't know.'

'You mean if he did you don't know?'

'I don't see the distinction.'

'What about you?'

'What about me?'

'Did you? Have affairs?'

'No.' Then, businesslike again, she said, 'Shall I go on?' Walker crossed his legs, preparing to resume his note-taking.

That evening he cooked dinner for them both. They ate outside, drank wine. He lent Rachel a sweater, which she draped around her shoulders. Earlier in the day he had seen her handwriting for the first time. Now, for the first time, he was watching her eat. Seeing things for the first time. Relationships last for as long as there are still things to see for the first time. Walker thought of the future when they would look back to the moment they first saw each other. She was eating lettuce with her fingers. A drop of dressing glistened on her lips. She dabbed her mouth with a napkin, blue. Her mouth.

They took the plates inside. Walker made coffee. Rachel had her back against the wall. She had discarded his sweater. He moved over to her, leant one hand against the wall, level with her shoulder. She took a dark gulp of wine, aware of his arm like the low branch of a tree she would have to duck under. Sleeves rolled above his elbows, veins in his forearm.

'That's a lovely dress,' he said.

'You like it?'

'Yes.' He moved his other arm so that it too was pressed against the wall on the other side of her shoulders and she was enclosed by the cage of his body, the hoop of his arms. The movement brought his face lower, a few inches closer to hers. Their lips were almost touching.

'You know what kind of dress that is?'

'The kind you can buy anywhere.'

'It's the kind of dress I want to put my hand up.'

She pressed back against the wall. Their hearts were beating faster.

'You know what kind of line that is?'

'No.'

'I think you do.'

'And that's not all,' said Walker. 'There's something else.'

'What?' The air felt heavy around them.

'It's the kind of dress . . .' Walker said, freeing the words from the coarseness in his throat, 'the kind of dress I want to pull up over your hips. The kind of dress where you raise your arms and I pull it over your head.'

'To do that the zip would have to be undone.'

Walker moved one hand from the wall to her legs, below the hem of her dress.

'After the zip was undone, then I would pull it over your head. Then—'

Walker moved his hand up between her thighs, feeling her skin become softer and softer until it attained that softness that can never be remembered because it is impossible to imagine anything so soft, because there is nothing to compare it with, to store it alongside. Their lips touched for a moment. Then Walker felt her hand on his wrist, pushing it away from between her legs.

'No,' she said, ducking beneath his other arm, smoothing down her dress. In prison he had heard stories like this many times, stories that ended in rape and hate. Walker took up the position Rachel had occupied, leaning back against the wall, his hands hanging by his side. She came towards him, kissed him on the lips.

'You understand?' she said.

'No.'

'But you understand?'

'No,' he said.

Malory lived—'as far as he lives anywhere'—in a beach house a couple of hundred miles up the coast. Rachel gave Walker a set of keys and he drove there the next day. A storm was building, the sun flinching in and out of clouds. The house was sparse and expensive, built mainly out of windows. Rugs on wood floors, white walls.

Despite everything Rachel had told him it was difficult to form an impression of Malory from the evidence of his home. There was furniture, a few records, books—not enough of either to suggest any passion for music or reading. There were a few pictures on the walls, none of which he paid much attention to— except for a framed Victorian photograph. It was of a man sitting in a chair, wearing a heavy sepia suit, eyeglasses. Walker wondered who it was and moved closer to read the small caption in the right-hand corner: 'Unknown Self-portrait'. Walker stepped back and gazed at the face of this strange ghost, captivated by the closed logic of the picture. Who was he? A man who looked like this . . . But who was he?

Walker moved away from the sad old photograph and went round the rest of the house. It was a place dominated by the absence of everything except light and places to sit or move around. In the study he went through Malory's files and desk. Rachel had said that if he was away his secretary came in once a week to take care of all his personal affairs, and in a desk drawer he found credit card statements and bills. From these he was able to trace his movements up until three months ago; since then there was nothing. The last payment was to a car rental firm in Durban. Walker made a note of the company's name and went round the house once more. No flowers or ornaments, only the vista windows looking out over the ocean heaving silently.

Back at his own apartment he called the rental company and asked if they had any information about a car rented three months ago by—

The woman cut him off there and said she couldn't possibly deal with queries like that on the phone. As soon as he put the phone down it rang beneath his hand: Rachel. Her voice.

'Did you find out anything?'

'Not really. What about this secretary—could I speak to her?'

'No point at all. She's been with him for fifteen years. He likes her because she never asks any questions. He won't have told her anything about where he is. Like I told you, he's a very secretive man. Pathological. You almost had to use the Freedom of Information Act to get his birthday out of him.'

'Yes.'

'So what will you do next?'

'I suppose I'd better start looking for him.'

'Meaning?'

'The only lead we have is that rental firm. I guess I'll head to Durban.'

'When will you leave?'

'As soon as I can.'

'But I'll see you before you go?'

'I hope so,' he said.

They met later that night, in a bar with candles and no music. Walker ordered beer, bought one for a guy he knew who was sitting at the bar. Rachel drank red wine that looked thick and sleepy

in the candlelight. In the curved darkness of her glass Walker
saw a reflection of both their faces, dancing, swaying, settled.
She handed him the documents that she needed Malory to sign.
Walker glanced through them.

'About money,' Rachel said.

'We can take care of that when I get back.'

'You're sure?'

'The money is no problem.'

Rachel finished her wine. 'Let's pay and go down to the sea,'
she said.

They walked to the beach, listening to the crash of waves. In
places the receding tide had left still pools of water that reflected
the stars so perfectly it seemed they were breaks of clear sky in
a beach of cloud. Jumping across them was like leaping over the
sky itself. Every now and then headlights from the coast road
probed out to sea. In the distance they could see the hazy spars of
the Bay Bridge. Clouds slipped past a moon that was barely there.
They threw a few stones into the sea, listening out for the faint
splashes. A ship's lights blinked in the middle of the darkness and
then disappeared.

'And nothing is but what is not,' said Rachel.

'Was that a quote?'

'Shakespeare. I forget which one.'

'William probably,' said Walker.

They sat and waited, looking out at the dark ocean. Rachel
said she should be getting back. Walker turned towards her.

'I have a present for you,' she said. 'Here.' She held out her
fist and dropped a thin silver chain into Walker's palm.

'Maybe it will bring you luck,' she said. 'Keep you safe.' Walker
remembered a comic strip he had read as a kid: 'Kelly's Eye'. As

long as Kelly wore this jewel around his neck he was indestructible. Each week ended with him walking out of an incredible explosion or twenty-car smash-up, naked except for the stone around his neck and a tattered pair of shorts which were also indestructible.

'Let me put it on for you.'

Walker bent his head and felt her arms reach around his neck, fiddling with the clasp. Her mouth was near his. This was the moment when they could have kissed but it passed.

'Do you like it?'

'Yes. Sorry, I never know what to say when I'm given a present.'

She smiled—'Let's get going'—and they began making their way back up the low cliff to her car.

'There's something else as well,' she said when she had unlocked the car door. She reached over to the passenger seat and handed Walker an envelope. In it was the photo that had been taken at the party. Or part of it anyway: it had been cut in two and the half he held showed Rachel, almost in profile, holding the wine glass in both hands as if she were praying.

'To remind me you exist?' Walker said.

'Maybe.'

'What about the other half?'

'I keep that. To remind me that you do,' she said. 'Can I give you a lift?'

'No. It's five minutes from here, that's all.'

They were both eager to be on their own now, wanting the leaving to be over with, knowing that everything between them would have to wait.

'Is there anything else I can do?' Rachel said finally, standing by the open door of the car.

'No. I'll call you.'

'Be careful, won't you?'

Walker said yes, yes he would. He watched her drive off and waited for the tail lights to disappear from sight before heading home himself.

IT WAS A THREE-DAY DRIVE TO DURBAN AND WALKER SET OFF THE next day. He crossed the Bay Bridge and headed up the coast. He had just passed Malory's house when a white mist rolled in from the sea, enveloping the road. He slowed to a crawl, winding down the window and feeling the air clinging damp to his skin. The mist thinned and he looked out at a zinc sky, pale sea rolling calmly on to white sand, grey-white gulls dotting the beach. When the mist closed in again, all he could see was the lighthouse glow of cars heading towards him.

He turned inland ten miles later and the mist cleared, the landscape becoming gradually flatter. That night he slept for a few hours in the car before pressing on, stopping only for food and gas. At first he listened to music continuously, but soon the radio began to irritate him and he drove in silence.

By now the landscape was flat and featureless, almost an abstraction, existing only as distance. A hundred years ago there had been no road, only emptiness; now there was a four-lane freeway but the road altered nothing, not the sky yawning over it or the land stretching away to the horizon. If walking was a form of thinking, then driving was a form of meditation or self-hypnosis which, instead of concentrating the mind, encouraged it to float. The residue of concentration required to keep the car on the road lent these drifting thoughts a sense of urgentless purpose.

Often, glancing in the driving mirror, he expected to see Rachel's face looking back at him.

He spent the second night in a motel and arrived in Durban late the following afternoon. The rental agency was on the edge of town. It felt strange, walking in after so long bent up in the car. There were no other customers and the man he spoke to had no objection to finding out about the car rented three months ago by Malory. He rifled through a filing cabinet, squinting through glasses that seemed to do his eyes no good at all, and came back with a sheaf of photocopied papers.

'According to this,' he said, 'the car was checked in at a rental firm in Kingston—not one of our offices—a small firm we have an agreement with. Our cars can be left with them and they get 'em back to us.'

'How long ago was that?' said Walker. 'When was it checked in?'

'Couple a months ago,' said the guy, unwrapping a stick of gum, feeding it between his teeth.

Kingston was another long haul, on the edge of the Southern Wetlands. Walker drove for two days, weather coming and going, birds. Power lines rising and dipping alongside him. Sometimes overtaking the same car three times in a day.

The last three hundred miles ran flat through the swamp. Trees were the same colour as the road, as the sky. Moss drifted from swamp maples. Here and there were splashes of dull red, either in the trees or in the road, the smear of hit animals. Rain spotted his windshield, hardly even rain.

The rental office was a run-down place near the railroad. A sign on the counter said: 'If You Don't Smoke I Won't Fart'. The guy behind the counter was chewing on a sandwich. The reception area smelled of chicken; maybe a cigarette had recently been smoked there. Walker leant his elbows on the counter, waiting for the guy's mouth to empty.

'I'm trying to find out about a car that was checked in a couple of months ago.'

'What car?'

'A blue Mustang. Licence 703 6GH. It was dropped off here by a man named Malory.'

The guy wiped his fingers, screwed the serviette into a ball and chucked it away. 'Let's see. What was the date exactly?'

Walker told him and he hauled a wad of oil-smudged papers out of a drawer, sniffed, began thumbing through them.

'Yeah, it was checked in here.'

'Do you happen to know anything about the person who checked it in? Where he went or anything like that?'

'Let's see. I was working that day.' Walker waited for him to go on but instead the guy scrutinized him and said, 'You a cop?'

'No.'

'Tracker?'

'No.'

'Finder?'

'No.'

'Then what you want him for?'

'He's a friend.'

'Yeah?'

'Yes.'

'And what's he supposed to have done, this friend of yours?'

'Nothing. I just want to find him.'

With small variants Walker would have this same conversation many times in the months that followed. Strangely, the subsequent willingness to help of whoever he was talking to bore no relation to whether they believed him or not. The dialogue was an elaborate form of greeting, a formality. People couldn't care less what answers he gave but no one wanted to forgo this little introductory exchange.

The guy nodded, satisfied: 'Let's see, only a few cars were checked in that day. If I remember right, if it's the person I'm thinking of, he asked about a hotel.'

He paused, waited. This was another feature of the conversations of the next months: they all fancied themselves as Scheherazade, needed prompting before they would part with the next crumb of information.

'And you recommended one to him?'

'The Metropolitan.'

It was five minutes away, one of those places that had always looked like it had seen better days. Walker took a room there and chatted to the clerk, a boy in his teens who let him look back through the register, happy to oblige. Sure enough, Malory had stayed there, just one night.

Walker was too tired to pursue things further. He trudged up to his room and called Rachel. The machine was on. He listened to the message and hung up. Then he redialled. He listened to her voice again, asked her to call him at the hotel.

He drank a beer and flicked through the channels on TV. He watched part of a programme about the lost city of Atlantis and the latest attempts to establish its historical authenticity. The noise of aqualungs was making him fall asleep. He flicked off the TV and dreamed he was still driving, driving through places he'd never been, places that didn't exist, sunken cities whose streets were filled with waving reeds and darting fish.

In the morning he persuaded the clerk to dig out Malory's bill. A waiter spilt a tray of tea nearby and Walker moved aside to study the bill while a cleaner wiped the floor. All the details of Malory's stay were itemized: how much he'd spent on dinner and drinks; even an account of long-distance calls. Malory had made two calls, both to a number in Meridian. He tried calling from the reception phone but the number had been disconnected. He made a note of the number and thanked the clerk. As he made his way from the desk someone touched his elbow.

'Walker?'

'Yes.'

'I'd like to speak to you for a moment.'

They walked away from the desk, stood near a plant offering a version of shade.

'You're looking for Malory.'

'I didn't catch your name.'

'Carver.' There was no handshake. Walker had never met him before but felt certain he recognized him from somewhere. Glancing down he saw that Carver had left a trail of dark V-patterned footprints from the spilled tea.

'Like I said, you're looking for Malory.' Knowing that some kind of response was called for, Walker did nothing, waited for him to continue. 'I'll put it differently. I know you're looking for Malory.' He waited but Walker waited longer. 'Do you know where he is?'

'If I knew where he was I wouldn't be looking for him.'

'But you are looking for him?'

'I just wanted to clarify a point of logic.' Carver looked at him patiently.

'Do you know where he is?' he asked at last.

'Why do you want to know?'

'You have any idea where he is?'

'You haven't answered my question.'

'If you hear anything, call this number,' he said, pulling a battered playing card from his pocket—a ten of spades. He scribbled on the card and handed it to Walker. Walker kept his hands in his pockets. Carver tucked the card into his breast pocket. Walker began to move away. Carver blocked his path.

'I'm talking to you.'

'No you're not.' Walker moved around him but Carver gripped his arm, hard. They were the same height.

'Did you hear what I said?'

'No.' Walker tugged his arm free.

'Let me give you a piece of advice, Lancelot. Everything she said to you was shit. Everything you hoped she was saying was shit. You think you have to go through all this shit just so you can fuck her?'

Walker concentrated on not moving, on letting nothing show.

'You want to learn the hard way, don't you?' said Carver.

'I don't even want to learn.'

This time Carver let him walk away. He had only gone a couple of steps when Carver called out after him, 'Hey, Lancelot!'

Walker kept moving and a second later something landed quietly in front of him. He looked down and saw a thin chain coiled up on the floor like a silver snake. He was able to check the urge to pick it up but, involuntarily, he reached up to his neck to check that his own chain was still there. Then walked towards the lift, the chain like grit beneath his foot.

Back in his room he crammed Carver's words to the back of his mind, concentrated instead on the question of how he had known who and where he was. It was possible that he had just been followed here—but it was more likely that Rachel's phone had been tapped. And the chain . . . Abruptly he remembered why he had recognized Carver: the party, the guy he had bumped into. He picked up the phone to call Rachel and put it down again immediately. He could feel sweat trickling down his ribs, a nerve twitching in his jaw. All this shit just so he could fuck her. He hurled the phone across the room. Looked around for something else to smash but instead sat down abruptly. Forced himself to stay perfectly still, slowly emptying his mind of everything. He remained like that until he had lost any sense of time, began to lose any sense of being the agent of his thoughts. Then, in the ensuing vacancy, he allowed his thoughts to re-form, focusing purely on the practicalities of picking up Malory's trail, on nothing else.

The lead was a flimsy one: the phone number from Malory's hotel bill. He dialled again—amazingly the phone still worked—but, as before, got the high tone indicating it had been disconnected. His only option was to trawl through the phone book for Meridian until he found the address. He had nothing else to go on.

A post office near the hotel had directories from all over the country. The directory for Meridian was one of the thickest in the rack. The only way to go about it was systematically. He found an empty table and got started. It was mind-numbing work, requiring an appalling amount of concentration, more boring than anything he had ever done. After two hours he got to G. The law of averages meant that he should find the number before M. Most likely he would get to it at W. His eyes felt like a microscope. If his thoughts wandered off he went back a couple of columns and resumed his trudge through the book, forcing himself to think of nothing.

He found the number under M, under the name of Malory: Joanne Malory. He cursed himself for his stupidity in not looking there first. Checked three times, unable to believe that he had found it, then jotted down the address. Back at the hotel he lay on the bed and shut his eyes, columns of numbers marching through his head. He dozed and dreamed of numbers.

The telephone woke him—the manager of the hotel wanting to know if he was staying another night. It was six o'clock, way after check-out. Walker stared at the digits on the telephone, adding them up across and down. Apologized, said he was leaving immediately.

It started raining sixty miles out of town. An hour later the rain was falling so heavily that it was impossible to see the road ahead. One wiper had given up and twitched helplessly in the downpour. Walker bent forward, peering through the windshield at a truck swimming towards him. The windshield was ablaze with light and then, as the truck passed, there was a blind drench of spray. He braked and felt the car slither, the wiper clearing a segment of visibility.

He must have missed a sign or taken a wrong turning: either way he was lost. He clutched the wheel with one hand and skimmed through the radio, hoping for some kind of confirmation of where he was. An old song came and went in a sea-spray of static.

He twisted the dial a fraction and a chubby voice said storms were ravaging the region. Storms and gale-force winds. Police advised people to stay home unless absolutely necessary, to drive with extreme caution. Several rivers had broken their banks, many minor roads in the region were flooded, the something bridge was down. The main roads between Belford and Oakham, Queenstown and Nelson, Darlington and Sable were closed.

These names meant nothing to Walker. No mention was made of Meridian or Kingston. The way the announcer talked of 'the region' without specifying which region, made him feel more lost than ever, as if he were nowhere, not even in the middle of nowhere, on the *edge* of nowhere, stranded between nowhere towns. The voice announced that we would now return to 'Melody through Midnight' and Walker snapped the radio off.

Lightning jarred the darkness. There was a long silence, so long it seemed the silence itself was waiting, and then thunder crashed all around. Easing through a curve he felt both right-side wheels bump off the road and begin dragging the car into whatever lay beyond. He hauled the car back on to the road but minutes later the same thing happened again—with the right wiper gone he could see nothing of what was happening over that side. It was dangerous to keep going and even more dangerous to stop: the first car to come by would plough straight into him.

He glanced down at the fuel gauge. Depending on the gradient the needle swung between the red strip indicating things were getting bad and the E indicating they couldn't get any worse. The rain eased off and then came pounding back, harder than ever. Here and there the road was flooded and the car plunged through the waiting lakes. He moved his face closer to the windshield as the road curved left. Immediately beyond the bend a tree was lying half across the road. He veered round the trunk and crashed through flailing branches. Lightning jagged down towards a church or tower in the distance.

Later, long after he had given up hoping for such a thing, he drove past a turn-off and signpost. He slid to a halt and backed up. The rain was so heavy he had to wind down the window to make out the sign, startled by the noise of the storm hammering on the roof, hissing. Seventy miles ahead was the town of Flagstaff; ten miles off to the right was a town called Monroe. He cranked up the window, turned right. Even ten miles seemed optimistic: for the last twenty minutes the needle had been stretched out horizontally, only momentarily twitching from E. The engine was sounding worse and worse. By the outskirts of Monroe it was like the last drops of Coke being sucked through a straw.

He drove into town along the main drag, past the waterlogged forecourt of a darkened gas station. Black ponds had formed around every drain, sometimes stretching from one side of the street to the next. A faulty light in a shop blinked off and on. He parked opposite the only place that was open, the Monroe Diner. Killed the engine and listened to the rain, the wind creaking through signs. He pulled a coat from the back seat and cracked open the door. The rain sounded like fat frying in a pan. He plunged his foot into a puddle and levered himself out of the car. Waded across the street.

Every face turned on him as he entered, the glare that passes for welcome in bars all over the world. He felt like a traveller who stops at a tavern in Transylvania and asks if anyone knows the way to Castle Dracula. Shook his hair and rubbed his feet on the crew-cut mat. Behind the bar a woman was pouring beer into an angled glass.

She smiled 'Hi' as he perched himself on a stool by the bar. 'What would you like?'

'Hi. Coffee, please.' Even before he asked for it, coffee was implicit in the idea of shelter offered by the diner.

Once he was sat at the bar no one took any notice of him. His hair dripped on the counter and into his coffee. He ordered food, looked around. A dozen people, mostly alone or in pairs. Every now and again the window bleached white by lightning. The barwoman brought his food, asked where he was heading.

'I'm on my way to Nelson,' he lied reflexively. 'I got lost in the rain some way back.'

'That's what it's like this time of year. Never rains but it pours. Never pours but it floods. And it always rains.'

'And you have rooms here?' Walker was scooping up his food American-style, using just the fork, talking and chewing.

'For one? For one night?'

'Yes.'

'That's no problem. Matter of fact, it wouldn't be a problem if you wanted rooms for eight people for a week.'

Walker paid for everything and took a beer upstairs. The room was on the top floor. He spent twenty minutes standing under a shower that was not quite hot enough, then sat on the edge of the bed, drinking beer and thinking about tomorrow, wrapped in a towel. Clothes drying over a fan-heater.

He finished the beer and walked over to the window, the town hunkered down under the rain. A car eased along the main street, slowed, pulled into the parking lot beside the diner. Walker flicked off the light and went back to the window. The car had disappeared from sight but he could see puddles stained red by the tail lights. Then the lights were switched off and there was the slam of doors opening and closing. He pulled on his clothes, warm from the heater, damp. He tossed a few things from the bathroom into his holdall and moved out into the corridor, locking the door behind him. A sign said EMERGENCY EXIT. It had not been used in a long time and he had to wrench it noisily open. The fire escape was behind the neon welcoming you to the Monroe Diner. He pulled the emergency door shut and zigzagged down the rusted steps. Rain purpled and greened around him. Hanging from the lowest rung he dropped to the wet tarmac. He moved round the parking lot to the car he had seen from his window. By now they would be on their way up to his room. All the doors were locked. He scanned the ground, found a large stone. Lightning flashed lazily. When the thunder came he hurled the stone through the driver's window. As he opened the door the interior light flashed on for a moment, a dim echo of lightning. He swept glass from the seat, pulled the ignition wires from the steering column. As soon as he touched them together the engine sparked into life.

He edged round the diner and out on to the rain-slick street. Two hundred yards down the road he flicked on the headlights. In a film now, he thought to himself, someone hidden in the back seat would put a gun to his head and whisper, 'Freeze.' Suddenly nervous, he looked over his shoulder, almost disappointed to find no one there.

Wind and rain howled through the broken window. He was chilled from his damp clothes. Twenty miles out of town he pulled over and clambered awkwardly into a sweater and jeans. He stretched the wet shirt over the broken window. It bulged and sagged and made no difference, but with dry clothes and the heater blowing he felt better.

As soon as he was warm he became sleepy. When he felt himself nodding off he slapped his face and turned off the heater until he was cold and alert, miserable again. Alternating between shivers and yawns. There was no question of stopping—he had to put as much distance as possible between himself and Carver before morning. Assuming it was Carver. He went over the scene back in Monroe and realized that for all he knew the occupants of the car were simply travellers who had decided to rest up for the night instead of pressing on through the storm. Rather than being a stroke of luck that he had been at the window as the car drove in, it could equally have been whatever was the opposite of a stroke of luck—he was too tired to think of the word, maybe there wasn't one—that they came along when they did and set off his paranoia like an alarm. Shit! He pounded the steering wheel and accidentally sounded the horn. He reassured himself by playing the scene over again, this time focusing on his reactions—on how it hadn't occurred to him even for a moment that the car hadn't come for him. Even if they didn't convince, the double negatives at least obscured the issue. Anyway, there was no going back. There was no going back but either way, he thought, going back over the same question again, he should get rid of the car as soon as he could—but wherever he left it it would still point in his direction. As soon as they found the car, any lead he had built up effectively counted for nothing—but he couldn't abandon the car in an unfindable place without marooning himself. The relentless orbit of thoughts tired him but at least, he reasoned, setting off the whole process again, at least it kept him from falling asleep.

The rain showed no sign of letting up. When he could barely keep his eyes open he pulled off the road and squelched up a narrow lane. He turned off the engine, climbed over the seat and curled up in the back.

Rain hammered on the roof of his dreams.

HE WAS WOKEN BY THE ALARM OF BIRD CALLS, A WET SUN SQUINT-ing through branches. He opened the door and pissed yellow into the trees. All around was the slow drip of last night's rain. His mouth was dry and he cupped a few drops in his hand to moisten his tongue.

He touched the loose ignition wires and the engine came to life immediately, heaving clear of the suck of mud. Back on the road the sun shone hard through the windshield. In the distance was a blue line of mountains.

A sign said MERIDIAN 120 MILES. The highway glistened.

Meridian, as the thickness of the phone book had suggested, was a big city. He drove downtown and parked the car beneath the track of the elevated train. It was a perfect spot to leave the car: abandoned vehicles were strewn all around, many already stripped down to rusty frames as if picked clean by vultures. Walking away he looked into the back of a burnt-out station wagon and noticed the remains of a road atlas: a core of red high-ways, smoke-grimed, becoming charred, leading to ashes.

He bought coffee and a street plan. Rampart Street was eight stops along the line but after so long in the car he preferred to walk. He followed the El, walking beneath the giant concrete legs that strode through the city. The sun streamed through the track, crosshatching the ground with shadows. Patches of sky blazed through the angles of wood and metal. Every ten minutes a train thundered overhead, obliterating everything. In his childhood the future had been depicted in terms of white capsules zipping noiselessly along rails suspended over the efficient life of a gleaming city. What had actually resulted was graffiti-mottled trains rattling over a landscape of rusting vehicles that no one wanted.

Rampart was a dilapidated street running parallel to the El, a couple of blocks to the south, number seventeen a faded one-storey place. A green-and-yellow FOR RENT sign added colour. He tried the bell and waited. A bird, bright as a goldfish, was perched on the phone line. Walker clambered over a fence and made his way round the back. Wooden steps led up to a door which opened when he tried it. He looked around and moved inside, shutting the door behind him, eyes adjusting. A tap dripping. He walked through the kitchen and into the hallway. Mail was piled up by the front door, junk mostly, a couple of letters and—he recognized the handwriting instantly—a card from Malory. Two lines: 'Hope this reaches you before you move. Thanks for everything.' Unsigned, postmarked Iberia, the date too smudged to read.

There was nothing in any of the ground-floor rooms. Upstairs, the bathroom cabinet was empty except for a yellow beaker. His face in the mirror was pimpled with mould. There were two bedrooms, one with a bare double, the other with a single and an old desk. When he opened a closet metal hangers jangled briefly. A tingle of déjà vu. He shut the door and opened it again, hoping he could define the sensation more exactly but this time there was nothing.

The desk drawers smelled of graphite. Paper clips, a broken pencil, blank pages of paper. He sat on the bed, forearms resting on his legs, hands dangling between his knees, one foot tapping out the pulse of a thought. He lowered his head, ran his fingers through his hair. As he did so he noticed, behind his feet, almost under the bed, a micro-cassette case. There was a tape inside but, except for the manufacturer's label, no indication as to what was on it. He pocketed the tape and peered beneath the bed on his hands and knees. The only thing there was a dusty magazine open at an article about the cathedral in Nemesis, a photo of a stained-glass window.

He went through the house again, unable to form any idea of what Malory might have been doing here. Tightened the tap as hard as he could, stopping the drip. Then let himself out of the back door, locking it behind him.

Out on the street a dog padded by. Its tail, balls, and ears had all been clipped off, giving it the wicked, harmless look of a medieval gargoyle. From a pay phone on the corner Walker called the number of the real estate agent on the sign. Thinking he was considering renting the place—'the property'—they were very friendly until he asked if they had any information about the previous tenant. They lost interest immediately and Walker had to move quickly to hang up before they did.

Near the El station he stood indecisively in the sunshine. Hitched his bag over his shoulder and said, quietly, to himself, 'So . . . What shall I do?'

Cars glinted past. What *could* he do?

He bought a ticket and walked up to the platform as the El train pulled in. It rattled past crumbling verandas, painted stoops, the open windows of kitchens and bedrooms. Water towers were visible in the middle distance. On old walls, the faded ghosts of advertisements.

The mainline train to Iberia didn't leave for an hour. He walked a couple of blocks from the station and saw a massive crane looming over the city. In a cut-price electronics store he bought a micro-cassette recorder. Stepping outside he looked up and saw the crane arm swinging round—though it took him several seconds to express it in these terms for he experienced the movement of the crane as a sensation rather than a perception. In that burst of panic he felt the air reeling—centrifugal, sickening—as if the crane were stationary and the street spinning around it, like a fairground ride or a record on a turntable. Then the correct relationship of stability and motion re-established itself, with the crane arm sweeping above the street. He tried to re-evoke the earlier sensation but now reason was firmly entrenched again and would not be caught off balance by something it knew to be an illusion. The experience disconcerted him all the same. If things could be sent reeling so easily, if momentarily, it would take only a slightly more elaborate arrangement of effects to throw the world more radically out of kilter.

Back at the station he tried the tape he had found earlier. He listened for a few minutes, turning the volume up and then fast-forwarded to a new section of the tape and listened again. Nothing. He fast-forwarded again, pressed play and listened to the hiss of the tape moving. He fast-forwarded to the end, turned the tape over and listened again. The same. Blank, the tape was blank. Shit.

Still with time to kill, he called Rachel. When she answered he could hear music playing in the background, a cello or double bass.

'Walker! I've been hoping you would call,' she shouted. 'Hang on, let me turn the music down.'

The music stopped and she came back a few moments later. 'That's better. Now I can hear you.'

'What was it, the music?'

'A Bach cello suite. You know it?'

'I don't think so.'

'It's my favourite piece of music. I'll play it for you when you come back.'

'You can play the cello?'

'I can play the record. We'll listen to it together.'

Her words triggered a memory that lay far in the future, when they were old and wood-smoke music drifted through the rooms of a home.

'Meanwhile,' said Rachel.

'Meanwhile, any news?'

'People have been asking for you.'

'A guy called Carver?'

'No.'

'Have you ever come across a man called Carver?'

'No.'

'You're sure?'

'Of course I'm sure. Why? Should I have done?'

'No, it's—it doesn't matter. What about the people who called round, did they give any names?'

'No.'

'Any idea who they were? Trackers? Finders?'

'I'm not sure.'

'Did you tell them anything?'

'No.'

'What about Joanne Malory?'

'Joanne? She's Alex's sister but he hadn't seen her in ten years. He had no contact with his family. She could have been dead for all Alex knew. Why, have you found her?'

'No, not really . . .' Walker paused and heard Rachel say, 'There is something though. A photo of Alex arrived in the post.'

'In the post?'

'Yes. This morning.'

'Where from?'

'It could be from anywhere. I mean it's impossible to say. You know sometimes a letter arrives without being franked? There's a stamp on it but no postmark.'

'What about the photo?'

'It's strange. Blurred, very grainy. It looks like it's been blown up from a larger photo.'

'Any sign of where it was taken? Or when?'

'None, I'm afraid, But you want to see it, yes?'

'Yes but . . . I'll have to call again. I'll try and find a place you can cable it to. I'm going to—' He stopped himself abruptly.

'Where are you going?'

'Listen, I'll call you again.'

'Are you OK?'

'Yes. Anyway, I've got to go.'

'Be careful.'

'You too.'

They waited for each other to say good-bye and then hung up.

It was a long, slow journey to Iberia. As the grimy landscape slipped past, Walker tried to take stock of what was happening. He was confused by Malory's apparently random movements across the country. Unless he was fleeing from someone or searching for something they made no sense—and even then they made little. And the trail ahead was fainter than ever. At first he had had addresses, then a phone number, now only a postmark. What next? The rhythm of the train was making him sleepy. He nodded off and woke painfully twenty minutes later, his head lolling from the edge of the seat like a dog's tongue. Across the aisle a woman had spread a blanket and a pack of tarot cards over her lap. As far as Walker could work out she was playing a kind of patience. The nearest card to Walker, the one that caught his eye, showed a tower struck by yellow arrows of lightning. Men and masonry tumbling to the ground. Realizing that he was looking, the woman smiled at him and said, 'It passes the time.'

Walker smiled back. He shifted uncomfortably in his seat, looked through his reflection at the nothing-happening landscape.

IN IBERIA HE BOOKED IN AT THE HOTEL RECOMMENDED BY A TAXI driver. He called Rachel, gave her the hotel's cable number and half an hour later held a copy of the photo in his hands. It was grainy, blurred and in transmission the image had deteriorated still further. As she had said, it was obviously an enlarged segment of a larger picture and from the few background blurs it was impossible to gain any clue as to when or where it was taken. It showed Malory in three-quarter profile: fortyish, short hair, the down-curving mouth of a man who had to make an effort to smile. Although more or less as Rachel had described him, Walker's initial reaction was one of surprise: he had not pictured Malory like this, this was not the impression he had built up. Almost immediately, though, his impressions began rearranging themselves in accordance with the image in his hand and the harder he tried to focus on this discrepancy between what he had been led to believe—or what he had come to expect—and what the photo showed, the more difficult it became to disentangle what he had imagined from what was revealed.

Even with the photo he was no better off than before in terms of what to do next. Malory could be anywhere for all he knew—another city, another country. He had nothing to go on. Hunting out the woman with the tarot cards to see if she could give him a few leads seemed as good an idea as any. Or flip through the phone book for a spiritualist who could offer guidance from beyond the grave.

Absurd though they were, these thoughts marked a turning point—the beginning of a turning point—in his search for Malory. From then on the nature of the search began subtly to change and he came to rely less on external clues than on his intuitive grasp of what Malory might have done in similar circumstances. He only understood this later. At the time he simply remembered the taxi driver saying, 'All tourists stay there,' when recommending the hotel. Probably this meant the taxi company had a deal with the place and received a percentage on everyone sent there. There was only one train a day from Meridian; no buses. So if Malory had taken the train he would have arrived at the same time of day as Walker and may have been referred to the same hotel. He went down to reception but they had no record of past guests and too many people passed by for them to recognize Malory's picture. Walker returned to his room and thought about what Malory would have done if he had been here. Probably he would have lain around like Walker was doing now, turning the TV on and off, getting hungry. Gone out to get a bite to eat, found a bar.

Walker looked out of the window. Dark, beginning to rain. He pulled on his jacket, folded the photo of Malory into his pocket, and went out in search of a bar. Across the way was another street which, from the quantity of neon shimmering through the rain, looked more hopeful. The neon, it turned out, was in the window of a shoe repairer's, a pharmacy, and a travel agency. Walker continued to the end and turned into a street crowded with people and cars. Two blocks along was a subway station and a man selling umbrellas. Feeling rain drip down his neck, Walker splashed across the road and bought one, asked if there was a bar nearby—a place where he could get a drink, something to eat. The umbrella seller directed him to Finelli's, a couple of blocks away.

Walker took a seat at the bar and ordered a beer, catching glimpses of himself in the mirror behind tiers of spirits. After another beer he ordered a burger and by the time that arrived he was ready for more beer. A sport he had never seen before was on TV. Mainly it involved fouling members of the opposite team and trudging off to the dugouts at the edge of the arena. As far as he could make out the game was divided not into halves or even quarters but into sixteenths and the score—unless he had misunderstood—was 540 to 665.

Walker turned to the guy next to him and asked about the game. He was thick-set, missing a couple of teeth and wearing a check work shirt, happy to converse in the peculiar idiom of booze—telling and never asking. This was fine by Walker, especially when it turned out that he came to this bar every night after work, regular as clockwork. Hour of overtime and in here by eight o'clock five nights a week.

'What about the other nights?'

'Those nights I get here a little earlier,' he laughed, coughing. They shook hands; the guy told him his name was Branch.

'Ever been tempted to trace your roots?' asked Walker. His new drinking companion didn't bother laughing. Walker bought Branch a beer, still sniggering quietly at his joke. Branch showed no sign of buying him one back so Walker ordered a couple more and asked if he happened to remember speaking to a friend of his who'd come here a couple of months back when he was in town.

The friend, as a matter of fact, who'd recommended this bar to him, he said, and went on to describe Malory.

Branch stopped chewing and siphoned off half his beer. Bar conversations were like this: sometimes it was difficult to tell if the person you were talking to was deep in thought or sinking into a stupor.

'Yeah. Maybe I do recall him.'

'Actually, I might even have a picture of him. Yeah, here you go. I've been carrying this picture around for months and never quite threw it away.'

Branch held the paper like he was gripping a fellow by the lapels.

'About two months ago, was it?'

'Exactly. To the day practically.'

'Yeah, I remember him.' He handed back the photo. 'We spoke a while.'

'What about—I mean, do you happen to remember what you spoke of?'

'Pretty much what everybody talks about.'

'Did he—I don't suppose he mentioned where he was heading to, did he?'

'Matter of fact he did—if it's the fellow I'm thinking of. Or leastways he asked if I knew when the bus to Usfret left.'

'And you told him?'

'I told him there was only one every three days and he'd missed that. Told him the best thing he could do was take the bus to Friendship and get a bus from there.'

'Usfret, right. He must have been on the way to see Joanne, his sister.'

'Well, I don't know about that.'

'Did he say he was going to get the bus like you said?'

'Didn't say but he certainly seemed grateful for the information.'

'And did he say how long he was going to stay for or where he might go after that?' Walker was conscious that he was over-playing his hand, pushing too hard.

'How come you're so interested in him?'

'Oh, I just wanted to catch up with him.'

'Folks say that, it generally means he owes them money. Either that or they want to kill him.'

Walker laughed unconvincingly. 'Not me.'

'You a cop?'

'No.'

'Tracker, huh?'

'No, I'm just a friend. A friend on his way to Friendship,' said Walker: his second joke of the evening.

'Shit,' said Branch, not in anger or derision, just to bring this phase of the conversation to an end. Walker glanced up at the television: the score was up into four figures now. He bought Branch a final beer and hurried back to his hotel.

The desk clerk looked patiently through the bus timetables while Walker breathed beer fumes over him. Unlike Malory, Walker was lucky with the buses—one left straight for Usfret the next morning. He could even book a ticket right there, at the hotel. Walker said yes straightaway, then, when the ticket was half-written, told the clerk to hold on for a while, he had just remembered a couple of things he might have to do.

'No problem,' said the desk clerk, tearing the ticket wearily in two.

Back in his room Walker tried drunkenly to organize his thoughts, lurching from one possibility to the next. Getting the express meant that he would gain some time on Malory since obviously, assuming the guy in the bar was right, he had simply gone to Friendship to get the bus to Usfret. Looked at like that there was no point in going to Friendship. But . . . But if from now on there were going to be fewer and fewer external clues to go on, then he was going to have to rely more on thinking himself into Malory's shoes. In that case the more exactly he managed to repeat Malory's moves the easier it would be to duplicate the choices he had made. Tracking Malory was not going to be like a game of snakes and ladders where he could leap forward five places. He could do that but something he came across in those five missed spaces might prove more important than the one he landed on.

He phoned down to reception, told them to book him a ticket to Friendship. As he was getting ready for bed, sorting through his bag for his toothbrush, he came across the Dictaphone and tossed it on to the bed. Lying there a few minutes later, he switched on the tape. Nothing. He flipped the tape over and fast-forwarded, almost to the end, in case there was a brief message tucked into the last minute of tape. He turned down the volume so that the hiss was less pronounced and let it play noiselessly. Or not quite noiselessly . . . He switched off the machine, ejected the tape and inserted the blank cassette that had come with the machine. Pressed play. He listened for a few moments, ejected that tape and played the other one. Yes, there was nothing to hear but there was a distinct difference in the quality of the silence. It was not a blank tape but a recording in which there was nothing to hear, a recording of silence. He listened intensely and realized that the tape was not as devoid of noise as he had first thought. Certain noises were conspicuous by their absence: it had not been made in the countryside—there was no sound of birds, no hedgerow rustle. Fiddling with the bass and treble controls to minimize hiss but retain clarity of sound, he strained his ears to penetrate the ambient silence and hunt out the faintest hint of other sounds. It was strange and difficult, sitting there, trying to shut out the silence of the room in order to decipher the silence of the tape. Doubly difficult since straining his ears like this made him aware of the obtrusive sounds that composed the silence around him. The machine had come with a small set of headphones and with these he was able to cocoon himself inside the silence of the tape. He could hear a faint rattle, like blinds shifting in a breeze, a bell chiming in the distance, the swish and murmur of traffic, the gurgle of pipes, maybe rain.

He was so immersed in listening that the click of the tape coming to an end sounded like a door slamming.

IN THE MORNING, SLIGHTLY HUNG-OVER, HE CAUGHT A BUS TO Friendship. Having fulfilled his commitment to retracing Malory's exact route—pointlessly—he bought a ticket for the onward journey to Usfret.

The bus did not leave for several hours. He wandered round the city and then ate lunch in a café run by identical twins, one cooking, the other serving, both smiling the whole time. Someone had left a paper behind, folded inside out, exposing the crossword and classifieds. The crossword had been completed and the ferry times to Ascension had been ringed in a small display ad. Walker rearranged the pages and skimmed the main items while eating his food. The only article he read right through was about the reconstruction of a dead man's face. Several people had died in a fire at a railway station and one of the bodies had remained unidentified. From the remains a forensic expert had built an impression of what the dead man had probably looked like, right down to his hair style. Six months later no one had come forward to identify him. He had vanished and it made no difference, no one noticed: a man who didn't matter to anyone except himself, maybe not even to himself. A man who owed nobody anything.

Weighed down by eggs and grits, Walker left the café and headed back to the bus station. There was something strange about the city but he was unable to work out what. Then it came to him. There were no trees or pigeons or gardens. Yet all around were the sounds of leaves rustling and the beating of wings, the cooing of departed birds. He was so shocked that he stood at a street corner, listening. The effect was unsettling, less because it was so odd than because he was unable to decide whether it was depressing or uplifting: depressing because these things were absent or uplifting because, though absent, their sound remained. Thinking of the tape he had listened to last night he set the Dictaphone on a wall and inserted the blank cassette. Pressed record and let the machine soak up the sounds all around.

He had time, just before the bus left, to buy a pack of five blank tapes.

The bus station at Usfret was the size of a small city, a shanty town in its own right. Buses from all over the country converged and departed in a scene of relentless chaos. Buses roared in and out continually, drivers jockeyed for position, horns blaring. Conductors called and joked to each other, children who had climbed on to sell drinks leapt down into the dust, clutching crates of empty bottles.

Signs warned of pickpockets and every few moments Walker felt a body shove suspiciously into him. He asked where you could get taxis and a white-haired man, lacking a hand, gestured vaguely with his stump.

Walker set off in the general direction, not properly understanding where he was supposed to be heading. He needed a piss and found a toilet that smelled like the source of all epidemics in

history. Over the years the city had sprawled further and further
until it had ruined the surrounding land and this lavatory was a
microcosm of the same process. The toilet had become progressively more clogged with effluent until it had encroached on to
the floor, spilling out of the door and eventually forming ghettos
of excrement and toilet paper for yards around. Walker tried to
avoid looking but it was impossible to resist the conclusion that
everyone here had more or less chronic diarrhoea the whole
time: every conceivable kind of human shit was here—except that
which suggested the normal working of healthy bowels. Even to
piss here seemed as risky as drinking contaminated water. Everything was contaminated, even your sight.

He continued walking until he came to an area that seemed
almost deserted compared with the bedlam of the main station.
Old men levered themselves along on crutches. Dogs and men
nosed through sprawling mounds of rubbish. Strewn all around
were rusted tins, bottles, and rags. Rubbish had acquired the
permanence and character of architecture. There was so much
rubbish that the idea of litter meant nothing. The landscape was
made of litter—not defiled by it—and the litter was defiled by a
film of oil oozed over everything by convoys of buses. Even the
mud underfoot seemed composed of oil which had been compacted hard and pressed into the ground by the passage of time
and tyres, as if the process which formed it three million years
ago were slowly beginning again.

Walker had definitely come the wrong way: quite abruptly
there were no more buildings, only coaches heading off across
a wasteland of iron mud. It was strange that this sprawling city
should so abruptly give way to nothing. He had assumed that the
centrifugal crowding of the city had flung people to the edges,
but now he wondered if it weren't the other way round, if the

surrounding emptiness had not impelled people centripetally to the centre of the town. So elemental was the fear bred by that emptiness that people wanted to crowd together in the filth of the city. The more crowded and debased their circumstances the more reassured they felt, as if living five or six to a room were actually one of the comforts the city promised.

In obedience to exactly this impulse Walker began making his way back towards the station. The sky was brilliant blue. Groups of men stood round burning braziers as the hot sunlight of the afternoon began turning quickly to the chill of evening. Two turbaned men tossed dice on to a handkerchief spread on the ground. Walker asked where to go for a taxi and they pointed off to the left. Several times youths asked Walker if he needed help and he muttered that he was OK, moving away if anyone persisted in offering assistance. He tried to look as if he were at ease and knew exactly where he was going, but thieves the world over must have been so familiar with this routine he wondered if it were not a more useful ploy to look helpless, terrified, and lost. Perhaps then people would leave you alone. The only truly safe course was to have less than anybody else—but here everyone seemed worse off than everyone else. Even possessing a set of healthy limbs was to enjoy a position of relative privilege and therefore vulnerability.

He found the taxi rank on the edge of the station, next to a vast market. The driver was unwilling to leave until he had a full load of passengers and Walker sat wearily in the back of a dilapidated Mercedes, shoving himself a little further into the corner every time someone else climbed in. A woman was squeezed up next to him, clutching bags of bulging shopping. As the car turned a corner one of her bags spilled over and fruit and vegetables went rolling across the floor. Walker bent down to help retrieve things and saw that an egg box had come open and one egg had smashed over his shoe. As soon as he saw it he was overwhelmed by a feeling of giddiness. The woman apologized and began dabbing clumsily at his shoe with a clump of tissues. Walker forced himself to smile, insisted it didn't matter. He breathed deeply, opened and closed his eyes, waiting for this sudden surge of giddiness, of vertigo, to pass.

Once he had booked into a hotel Walker sent a letter to Malory. In fact he sent ten of them, putting blank sheets of paper in envelopes and sending them to him care of American Express in towns he may have passed through. On each of the envelopes he wrote 'Please forward if necessary'. If he had nothing else to go on—no idea of where Malory had gone next—he could stop at each of the towns and ask if there was any mail for him, Alex Malory. Nine times out of ten the letters would be waiting but occasionally, he hoped, they would have arrived at a place Malory had actually passed through. If the mail had been picked up, then Malory had been there between the letter's arrival and Walker's own. If they were sent to a place Malory had already left, it was possible that he would have arranged to have letters forwarded. In this way the letter served as a kind of tracking device, an advance scout.

Beyond that he had little idea what to do in Usfret, a dirty, crowded, sour-smelling town. He walked the streets looking for—for what? For a sign that Malory may have passed through, an indication of where he had gone. He felt pointless, absurd— and then, on his second day in the city, he saw Malory.

Walker was heading towards Americas Square in the middle of the city. As he got nearer to the square the streets became more and more crowded. In the Spanish quarter, where some kind of fiesta was in progress, it became difficult to move. That was as nothing, however, compared with the crush that Walker found himself in twenty minutes later in the area around the square itself. The streets here felt like the packed terraces of a soccer stadium. By the time Walker saw it was hopeless—that he would never get to the square—it was impossible to extricate himself from the crush; he could go only in the general direction of the crowd. In places—by the entrance to subway stations especially—the crowd had congealed completely. People trying to get out of the subway found the exit plugged by crowds attempting to come in. A woman lost her footing and disappeared from sight. It seemed certain she would be trampled underfoot but she emerged, ashen, weeping, a few seconds later.

The crowd was not uniformly dense and as long as you abandoned all volition and went where the crowd willed, a degree of movement was possible. After the crush around the food stalls Walker found himself in a less compacted part of the crowd. Stumbling through the undergrowth of feet which trod and tripped over his own, he took brief faltering steps. Up ahead a man was trying to manoeuvre his bicycle through the crowd—and there, right next to him, was Malory. The realization passed through Walker like a shock. It couldn't be but it was, he was sure. The very randomness of the sighting, the almost instinctive recognition, was virtual proof of that. Walker yelled out above the hubbub of the crowd, 'Malory!' A dozen faces turned round, Malory's among them. There was a brief surge and the faces turned immediately away. He yelled again and this time more people turned back—but not Malory, who seemed to be making an effort to move through the crowd. Walker shoved his way past the bodies in front of him. Malory was moving with the general flow of the crowd,

not straining to get ahead but maintaining a steady ten yards between himself and Walker. Elbowing his way more aggressively,
incurring curses and retaliatory shoves, Walker closed the gap
to three yards. Malory continued moving forward, so calmly
that the surrounding people would not have guessed he was trying to get clear of the figure barging and squirming behind him.
The calm was deceptive, for Walker saw now that every time a
slight gap opened in the crowd Malory used that opportunity
to gain a few yards' advantage. There was a ripple of shoving
and stumbling ahead of Walker and he saw Malory abruptly
stranded in a pack of bodies. The crowd formed contour lines
which had bunched themselves tightly around Malory, but Walker
was still able to move relatively easily. He barged through the
scrum of bodies, his arms coming clear of the surface of shoulders like a swimmer's. A wave of shoves passed through the
crowd. Malory tottered but people were packed so tight around
him that it was impossible to fall. Using his arms like a wedge
and then slipping into the gap, Walker moved within two yards
of Malory but here the crowd was so dense that no movement
was possible. Panic was spreading. There was another shove
from behind. Three people disappeared from sight, initiating a
counter-surge which sent everyone lurching in the other direction. Walker lost his footing but was immediately wedged upright
by the press of bodies from the other side. He glared round and
joined in the shouts of recrimination, aware that by elbowing
his way through the crowd he had helped set up the ripples and
currents of panic which were threatening to engulf him. Malory
was only a yard away. Walker's arms were pinned by his side; if
he could have raised them above the pack of people he could have
reached out and touched his shoulder. For five minutes they remained like this, the crowd like a vast millipede, swaying on tiny

legs which were always about to collapse beneath it. Surges and counter-surges rocked through the crowd until the crush began to ease. Malory moved a few steps and then another yard. Walker stumbled forward and then found himself penned in again. Moments later he was able to move, but all the time the distance between himself and Malory was increasing. It was like being in an ocean: currents and eddies, powerful riptides, sucked you in the opposite direction to that in which you wanted to go. This worked well for Malory, who moved whichever way the current took him, but for Walker it made the task of following him impossible. Where the crowd urged Malory in one direction, a few moments later it tugged Walker away in the other. Malory was ten yards clear now and it was impossible to beat a path through to him. There was another surge and Walker was swept further from Malory, forced to the other side of a row of parked cars. He felt a hard shove in the back. Stumbled and grabbed the shoulder of the woman in front, almost dragging her to her knees. He regained his balance and looked round but there was no sign of Malory in the spot where he had last seen him.

Monitoring footage of the scene, police gradually dispersed the crowd but Walker remained trapped for several hours more. By any normal standards it was still fantastically crowded but eventually he stumbled into his hotel, shocked by the empty expanse of the lobby.

He was exhausted, his muscles ached and his back and arms were bruised. Soaking in a bath he went over and over the day's events until he began doubting whether it was actually Malory he had seen. And even if it had been, Walker was now as far away from him as ever. The fact that he had been within a yard of Malory meant nothing.

These doubts were reinforced the next day when he called

Rachel. She had just spoken to a man in Port Ascension, a friend of Malory's who was sure he had seen him there.

'He wanted to know if I had a number for him.'

'How long ago?'

'I spoke to him this morning. Just a couple of hours ago. He left a number.'

Walker wrote the number down. 'And what was the name of the town?'

'Port Ascension. Do you think he might be there?'

'It's possible,' he said absently. Ascension . . . Ascension. He tried to place the name and then remembered: the ferry times in the newspaper. A coincidence—but without coincidence life didn't happen. Coincidence was destiny broken down into its smallest unit.

'Are you still there?'

'Yes, sorry.'

'You don't sound very optimistic.'

'I thought I saw him yesterday.'

'You saw Alex?'

'I'm not sure now. I could easily have been mistaken. The more I think about it the less sure I am . . . I think of you a lot.'

'I know. I'm smiling when I think of you, Walker.'

'What does that mean?'

'It means I like thinking of you.' Walker smiled into the phone. They listened to each other breathing. A few seconds later they hung up.

THE SEA WAS ROUGH, THE BOAT SMELLED OF OIL AND BAD FOOD. For as long as Walker could remember he had been disappointed by boats: something to do with the thickness of the metal, the size of the bolts; the way everything was covered in a thick skin of paint, the way you had to struggle through low self-closing doors, the way the toilets were always awash with water. He stood on deck and was surprised by how quickly he became bored watching the land receding, the frantic gulls. Even the sea was disappointing. Grey, cold.

He went below deck to get some food but everything looked too foul to eat. A smell of french fries and eggs emanated even from the Bolognese sauce congealing in a brightly lit tin. He wandered to the lounge where people were already asleep on the floor—the seats all had armrests to prevent people stretching out on them. No effort had been spared to make the crossing as miserable as possible.

Soon people were vomiting all over the ship. The smell of sick was impossible to dissociate from the reek of the food cooking in the galleys. Walker thought he might throw up himself and went back on deck. The air was full of spray. To the disappointment of those lined up at the stern, cameras at the ready, darkness fell without a sunset.

Walker remained on deck and took a sounding—as he suddenly, under the nautical influence, began to think of the recordings he made with the Dictaphone. Later, listening back to the recording, he was surprised to find how the sounds of gulls and wind, the slap of waves, evoked not the grim reality of the crossing but the romantic ideal of a sun-soaked cruise.

The boat docked at dawn the next morning. Walker joined a line of people shuffling towards immigration officials, borrowing pens to fill in disembarkation cards. 'Purpose of visit': Walker hesitated, scribbled 'Tourism' and gave the Grand Central Hotel—glimpsed over the shoulder of another passenger—as the place he would be staying. He waited at the yellow line until the port official waved him forward—the sullen, bored, omnipotent wave of frontier staff the world over. Walker said, 'Hi,' handed over his card, waited. Without looking up the guy consulted a huge logbook, let it fall shut and said, 'Over there.'

'What?'

'Wait over there.'

Over there was a bench. Walker waited ten minutes. A door opened and another guy, squinting at the papers in his hand, called out 'Mr . . . Walker?' as if the name were unpronounceably, suspiciously alien. Walker followed him into a room: desk, chair, banks of files. The guy smoked, was unshaven, wore an open-necked shirt. Walker recognized the uniform instantly—bribe—and this knowledge gave the subsequent interrogation a relaxed, veiled purpose. All questions about his circumstances and intentions were really intended to establish only one thing: how much he was good for. Walker indicated he might be good for plenty, especially if he could be furnished with a little extra assistance. The port official hesitated. That depended...

'A friend of mine arrived here,' said Walker, coming straight to the point. 'A couple of days ago, I think. I'd like to look him up. I need the address he gave on his disembarkation card.'

'Impossible.'

'How much?' Walker could see greed flickering in the other man's eyes and knew that in an hour he would be out of here with everything he needed. Only the price had to be finalized now.

It took even less time than he expected. He checked in at the Grand Central and dialled the number Rachel had given him. No answer. He tried later, again without success, and set off for the address given to him by his friend—as he now thought of him—at the port.

The house was in the middle of an old terrace of high town-houses in the east of the city. He stood in the lobby, waiting for the elevator, obscurely convinced that something was wrong. In the elevator he stared at his face in the mirror and wondered what he looked like. His reflection posed the question it was supposed to answer.

The apartment was on the seventh floor; by the fifth Walker felt certain he was making a mistake. The elevator stopped on the sixth floor. A cigarette-faced woman stepped aside to let Walker off. He padded along a corridor and up the emergency stairs. Easing the fire door open a fraction he had a good view of room 7D. He allowed the fire door to close until there was only a knife-edge of light. Waited.

After ten minutes a squat man emerged from the lift and knocked on the door. The door opened and he spoke quietly. Seconds later a figure Walker recognized as Carver emerged.

Walker moved back down the stairs but heard footsteps coming from below. As quietly as possible he trotted back up to the top floor. A folding-ladder led to a frosted skylight. The ladder squeaked as Walker pulled it down, creaked as he climbed up. He cracked open the skylight and clambered out on to the roof.

The noise of traffic was all around. Shadows hazed and disappeared. He crossed the roof and made his way along a ledge to the next house. There was a skylight here, locked from the inside. The next house along was higher than the rest and he had to haul himself up. As soon as he had done so he heard footsteps from behind. Keeping low he moved across the roof and ducked behind a crumbling chimney stack. Seeing his pursuers fanning out from the skylight, he scuttled away and lowered himself down on to the roof of the next house. He continued moving like this until the terrace was split abruptly by a service alley running between two houses. In the darkness below, dustbins and trash, the glint of broken glass. The gap was only four yards but a low ornamental wall at the edge meant that it was impossible to get the kind of run-up he needed. He glanced back and tried the entrance to the lift housing. It was locked, but lying nearby were two rusty scaffolding poles.

He picked up one of them, carrying it in his arms like a tight-rope walker, making his way to the edge of the building. Resting it on the low wall he began feeding the pole out over the alley. With a yard still to go it became too heavy to handle. He dragged it noisily back over the wall towards him and tried again, this time standing it on end and lowering it by degrees towards the opposite roof. When he could hold it no longer he let it drop like a metronome across the alley. It smashed down on to the low wall opposite, bounced, shivered. As he scrambled to steady it, the pole slipped off the far wall, flicked up from beneath his hands, and went twirling out of sight. By the time he heard the crash and tangle from the alley below he was already dragging the other pole into position, this time to a place where a gap in the wall would support it like an oarlock. He upended the pole, released it, and watched it swing down. Again it clattered and bounced but this time, anchored by the wall, it remained lodged on the far roof. He pushed it out until there was an overhang of a foot on each side and then climbed over the edge of the building, began moving out over the alley. A yard out he brought his legs up and curled them around the pole so that he could move more quickly.

There was a shout from the roof. Raising his head and looking back between his arms he saw his pursuers rush to the edge. They tried to prise the pole free of the gap in the wall but Walker's weight had jammed it in further. He continued moving, hand over hand, pulling with his shoulders, pushing with his legs, hauling himself away. He felt the pole quiver as they began heaving it free of the gap, followed by a jarring crash as they let it fall back on to the top of the wall. The impact shook his legs free and left him hanging by his hands. For a second he dangled uncontrollably and then, setting up a rhythm, began moving again, hand over hand. Glancing back he saw them standing on the wall, trying to tug the pole sideways, towards the edge. With a final heave they wrenched it the remaining inch and out over the alley. Walker made a grab for the building. The scaffolding pole whipped past his shoulder, sheered away beneath him. His fingers curled over the wall. Another crash from the alley below. He scrambled on to the roof and looked back. For a moment the four of them stood there, Walker and his three pursuers, not moving.

'Listen,' Carver called, pausing for breath. 'We should talk. We can help each other.'

Walker gulped in mouthfuls of air. Carver was talking again, silhouetted against a sudden burst of sunlight.

'We want the same thing. We know where Malory is.' Walker had got his breath back, was on the brink of listening. He turned and walked along the row of roofs. Carver was calling, 'Wait. Walker, wait.'

Walker kept moving, heard Carver shouting, 'This is your last chance, Lancelot. You're a dead man.'

Walker tried an entrance to the emergency stairs. It was locked but the frame and door were so rotten that one kick smashed a hole. He reached through and unlatched the door, lowered himself on to the steps. He charged down the stairs and out into the swarm and din of the street. A taxi pulled up nearby. Walker barged past a waiting executive and wrenched the door open, lunged in.

Back at the Grand Central he piled his stuff into a bag. His only concern was to get away from Ascension. Where he went next didn't matter. But even as he thought this he wondered also if flight might not be the best form of pursuit, the best way of finding Malory. Malory's movements were so random that perhaps he too should abandon any plan. He hurried to the station and bought a ticket to Alemain, the closest town to which he had sent his speculative mail.

He arrived at the station with time to spare: the train did not leave for fifteen minutes and passengers were not yet being allowed on board. He drifted round the concourse, half expecting to catch a glimpse of Carver. At least half the people here, it seemed, were either following or being followed. Perhaps it was so many people wearing hats that contributed to this impression. Anywhere else a hat looked like an affectation but here, in a railway station, it was part of the standard luggage of travel, a kind of ancillary ticket. The chance to wear a hat with impunity was probably one of the things that preserved the romance of train journeys.

As he made his way towards the platform he passed a Photo-Me booth and ducked beneath the curtain. It was as good a place as any to hide from view but, without intending to, he found himself spinning the stool down as far as it would go and paying in coins, posing for four sudden snaps of the flash. Clambering out of the booth he saw a woman reading a tabloid stroll towards him. An Asian girl went into the booth. He looked at the clock and at the sign that said 'Photos Delivered in Four Minutes'. All around this sign were sample photos of smiling couples, smiling and serious individuals. One strip showed a black and white couple kissing and pulling faces—you could do what you wanted in the relative privacy of the booth; the machine didn't care, it recorded but didn't notice. Ugly or beautiful, tall or short, everyone came out the same way.

After only a couple of minutes the pictures arrived. He moved towards the machine but saw they were of a woman, the woman reading the paper, who reached down and took them.

The developing times were cumulative, so he had another four minutes to wait—more like five probably—and it was now exactly four minutes to. The train's departure was being announced. Two minutes clicked by. He looked up at the clock, glanced down at the little metallic cage where the photos arrived and set off for the train. He had gone two steps when he thought he heard a faint rustle from the booth. He hurried back, checked the empty tray and ran for his train.

BUILDINGS, PEOPLE, STREETS, AND SHOPS: BEYOND THAT ALEMAIN had little to recommend it—especially since Walker had such trouble finding his way around.

He had picked up a street plan at the station and set off for the AmEx office. For an hour now he had been pacing the streets, scrutinizing the map at almost every corner, but was still no-where near his destination. The smaller streets were not shown on the map but it was detailed enough to reveal that he was lost. This was the true purpose of maps: without one it was impossible to say with certainty that you were lost, with one you *knew* you were lost.

Walker persisted for a long while, becoming steadily more frustrated as streets changed name, distances expanded or con-tracted and expected turnings and landmarks failed to appear. Gradually he became convinced that the map bore no relation to his surroundings. The fact that here and there reality and representation corresponded was entirely coincidental. It took Walker a long time to accept this: so entrenched was his faith in the integrity of maps that his first reaction was to assume that the map was right and the city somehow wrong. The whole point about a map was that it was a more or less accurate representation of reality. He had heard of towns where streets and buildings were being demolished and built so fast that maps, lagging behind reality, were obsolete by the time they were printed, but this map either deliberately distorted reality or ignored it.

He threw the map away and walked on. Once he had got used to the idea that the town was not as the map had led him to expect, it was surprisingly easy to find his way around.

At the AmEx office a pretty Chinese woman trotted off to look for his mail. A minute later she came back with the letter he had sent from Usfret. He thanked her and headed back to the station, caught the next train to Avlona.

He had noticed bicycles being wheeled on to the train at stations *en route,* but when it pulled into Avlona he was surprised at how many people had bicycles. As he walked towards the centre of town, cyclists were coming and going in all directions. All around was the angular flash and blur of spokes and frames.

It was a warm spring afternoon and Walker dawdled on his way to the AmEx office. Relieved to be somewhere pleasant after Usfret and Ascension, he decided to spend the rest of the day there, even though the letter from Usfret was waiting for him. He walked back out into the last sunshine of the day. Leaves fluttered like bunting.

Outside a bric-a-brac store he spun a squeaking rack of postcards. An old photograph of London caught his attention. It was taken in the nineteenth century when London was a teeming and bustling centre of commerce and trade—but the city was deserted. Walker puzzled over the image for several minutes before realizing that the long exposure time had emptied the scene of all moving objects: people, trams, horses.

He walked and considered what to do next, where to go. Again, when he looked back, this moment would represent another important shift in the nature of his search for Malory. For the first time he had formulated the question in terms of where he should go rather than where Malory had gone. It was not that the question of Malory's whereabouts no longer mattered—but that question had been absorbed so totally into his own decision-making process that he no longer needed to ask it. It was as if the only way of duplicating Malory's movements was to anticipate them. Inevitably he would make mistakes but these mistakes might lead him to the right track eventually. The right path might be, precisely, a culmination of mistakes, of detours. As soon as you recreated it on a map or set it down in a book, even the most idiosyncratic random movements acquired an internal logic; their purpose remained elusive but they formed a path, a route, led somewhere. With such a map he could find his way back.

In the morning he walked past a shop with a row of used bicycles chained up outside. The shop was run by an old man who claimed to have ridden in the Tour. Walker indicated a bike he liked and the old man unlocked the chain and extricated it from the row: ten-speed, dropped handlebars, light enough to be picked up easily with one hand. Walker rode it around the block and asked the old man what he wanted for it.

'You've read those stories about a knight on his charger?'
'Yes.'
'You seen Westerns? The cowboy on his horse?'

Walker nodded.

'Now it's you on that bike. A clear line of descent. Seventy-five buys you the bike and the ancestors.'

'What about just the bike?' said Walker, but as far as the old man was concerned the deal was clinched already.

Walker paid up, lashed his bag to the rack and pedalled off.

'So long, cowboy,' called the man who had once ridden in the Tour, stuffing Walker's money into his pocket.

The morning's chill still clung to the air but after riding for fifteen minutes he felt fine. He headed out of town, the volume of cyclists diminishing steadily as he went. The road was flat and ran alongside a river with fields stretching away on the other side.

For lunch he bought bread, fruit, and water and sat down to eat behind the goalpost of a deserted football pitch. A breeze rustled the bushes beyond the touchlines. The goal was smudged with dried mud where the ball had ricocheted off crossbar and posts. The goalmouth and centre circle were dry and bare, pock-marked by studs. Chewing and swallowing, he imagined some archaeologist of the future re-creating sequences of play and estimating the scores of games played here from the patterns of stud-marks on the pitch.

In the middle of the afternoon he came to a bridge, rising high and golden in the blue sky. As he drew closer he saw that what he had taken to be the ripple of hot air was actually the bridge itself rippling in the air. It undulated gently as if a wave were passing through it, as if its burnished girders were made not of steel but of some highly elastic material.

He stopped at the edge of the bridge, watching it rise and fall rhythmically, breathing. There was no traffic. A sign said BRIDGE CLOSED and a barrier blocked the carriageway. He manoeuvred his bike round the barrier and walked out on to the bridge. At first, although he could see the bridge undulating ahead of him, the cables growing taut and slack with strain, he hardly felt any movement. Then, as he moved out over the river, he felt the road shifting beneath his feet like a ship on calm seas. There was no sense of danger. He looked at the bridge's flowing reflection in the river below. He dropped a stone over the edge and watched it fall and splash, vanish. Out of the corner of his eye he saw a bird swoop down and glide low over the river. After a few minutes he got on his bike and cycled over the shifting hills and dips. The sun strobed through the stanchions and cables rearing above him.

When he had crossed to the far side he looked back at the bridge rising and falling in the blue air.

That night he slept by the roadside and cycled on as soon as the sun shuddered clear of the horizon. Late in the afternoon, his legs wobbly after so long on the bike, he rode into a city where there were no people, only streets—narrow, cobbled, crossed by even narrower streets that led to rain-damp alleys and dead ends. Torn posters advertised political meetings and sporting events. There were parked cars but no sign of the people who drove them. A few shops had their shutters pulled down but most were open for business as usual. As he opened the door of a pâtisserie a little bell rang like a wind chime. The shelves were half-empty with bread and cakes. He took a croissant that tasted as if it had been fresh-baked that morning. Took two more and walked out of the shop, still chewing, flakes of pastry falling to the floor. The street was divided sharply into sunlight and a tide of shadow inching towards the opposite wall. Riding along the cobbled streets was so awkward that he left the bike where it was, propped against the shop window.

He came to a large square. In the middle was a water fountain, a statue of a dragoon or fusilier wading through it, sword raised above his head. He wore a cloak, armour breastplate, and knee-length leather boots—under one of which was trapped a flapping fish: not a dragon or serpent but a playful and, apparently, un-distressed fish. Despite the raised sword there was no suggestion that this aggressive posture indicated any ill-will towards the fish. He just happened to be brandishing a sword and treading on a fish which squirmed good-humouredly beneath his feet, as if it were being tickled rather than squashed.

Walker dunked his head in the bubbling water, his face level with the bemused eye of the fish. Fingered back his wet hair, feeling the cold drips on his neck and shoulders. The shadows cast by the buildings on one side of the street climbed the walls of those on the other. He hoped to come across some indication of what had happened here but apart from the absence of people everything was completely normal.

Halfway down a street of expensive shops he went into a place called Hombre. He flicked through rows of jackets and trousers and then stripped off and unwrapped a pair of under-pants. Next he extricated a shirt from the pins, cardboard and cellophane and put that on, then a pair of cotton socks hanging on a rail. He tried on a suit jacket which fitted perfectly. The trou-sers were too big round the waist so he took a pair from the suit that was the next size down. He took his time choosing a tie, fi-nally deciding on one that was a sober grey with light spots. In the basement he found a pair of suede shoes with thick soles—comfortable, easy to run in. Back upstairs he picked out another shirt, extra pairs of underpants and socks, a sweatshirt, and a pair of cotton trousers which he crammed into a bag. His old clothes seemed like sour-smelling rags now and he dumped them in a bin.

As he was leaving he noticed the till. He pressed a few buttons and the cash drawer sprang open. He helped himself to a few notes and some change, pushed the till shut, and stuffed the money into a pocket.

Outside the street was flooded with shadow. Only the third storeys and above were still in the sharp-angled sunlight. Newspapers and bags of garbage were piled up, awaiting collection on the sidewalk. Nearby, rustling in the breeze, were lengths of film that had obviously overflowed from a dustbin. The further he walked the more film there was, coiling round his feet, twitching like two-dimensional snakes. He picked up one of the strips and held it up to the light, the brown shine turning immediately to brilliant colour. The film showed a man walking down an old street. All the other strips were blank or damaged: nothing to be seen. He coiled the original strip loosely around his arm and walked on until he came to a bar. Just inside the door was a flashing pinball machine. He walked round the bar and took a beer from the fridge, helped himself to a sandwich from beneath a glass lid.

Alternating between mouthfuls of beer and sandwich he hoisted himself on to the bar, feet resting on a stool. He held the film up to the light, squinted at the sequence of images. Peering closely he saw it was not a street but a bridge with elaborate decorations. The last few frames, as far as he could make out, showed the man stopping at a pay phone at the far side of the bridge. As soon as he put the length of film down on the bar it curled up reflexively like a threatened animal.

It was almost dark by the time he left the bar. Sleepy, unsure of his bearings, clutching his bag of clothes, he began looking for a place to stay the night. He ignored the smaller houses: in this unusual position he could treat himself to somewhere lavish. Now that it was evening the city seemed almost ordinary, like an especially quiet Sunday night when people had retreated indoors.

A telephone was ringing in the distance. As he turned a corner the ringing got louder: the pay phone across the street. The intervals between rings became longer and longer the closer he moved to the phone. It was unnerving, a pay phone ringing like this. One day there would be a superstition about how it was bad luck to pick up a phone ringing randomly. Superstitions needed centuries to establish themselves. He walked past the phone, resisting the temptation to answer, but the ever-expanding lasso of rings continued to encircle him as he moved away. He felt like he had refrained from waking someone in the grips of a nightmare. When he was almost out of earshot he hesitated, unsure if it was still ringing, and walked back towards the silent phone.

At the far end of a cul-de-sac he let himself through a groaning iron gate. A line of cypresses ran along the side of a path which stretched to a low wall at the other end of the garden. Too tired to investigate the grounds, he walked round the edge of the house. He came to a large patio with a sun umbrella and chairs. An open door led to a conservatory, full of plants he recognized but couldn't name: leaves, stems. He walked in through the humid air of the plants and into the house, cautious, still unused to this licence to go where he pleased. He peered into living and dining rooms and made his way upstairs.

The bathroom was exactly what he had hoped for: a large oval bath, thick towels hanging on chrome rails. Pink and green bottles of lotion gave the air a sweet sensual smell. He twisted the hot tap and steaming water cascaded immediately into the bath. In the bedroom next door he took off his new clothes and chucked them on the floor. On a bedside cabinet was a framed wedding photo: a couple on the steps of a country church, making their way through a snowstorm of confetti. At the edge of the photo was a woman he thought was Rachel, throwing confetti, laughing. Her hair was different, she looked heavier: impossible to tell for sure. Next to her was a man whose face was obscured by the blurred arm of another confetti-throwing guest.

Walker took the photo into the bathroom. The feel of hot water, fresh enamel on his back. Through the pebbled window he could see a square of dark-blue sky which, like the glass of the photo, was becoming saturated with steam. He dismantled the frame and took out the photo, hoping to find something written on the back. Nothing. He lay back in the dreamy steam of the bath, holding the photo in damp fingers, staring.

HE HAD NO IDEA OF THE TIME WHEN HE AWOKE: THE SHUTTERS were open but heavy curtains excluded the light which gushed in when he drew them back. He could see the red-tiled roofs of the town, washing lines and TV aerials. From here the buildings appeared jammed so closely together that there seemed scarcely to be any roads separating them. In the distance hills basked under a calm sky.

It was so bright outside that he walked into a pharmacy for a pair of sunglasses that made the faded pinks and oranges of the buildings flare up darkly beneath the brown-blue sky. There were details everywhere. It was impossible to miss anything. A NO LITTERING sign with lovers' initials scratched into the paintwork. A beer can crushed flat in the road. A shutter banging in the wind. A dust-smeared window. A spectrum-smeared puddle.

He came to a garage whose forecourt was crowded with second-hand cars. From the office he took several sets of keys, one of which fitted a red Ford. He manoeuvred out of the garage and drove to a grocery where he loaded up with provisions. Then, threading his way through the narrow streets, he headed out of town.

Soon he was driving along winding country roads. Hedges, fields sloping into distant hills, grazing clouds. Every couple of miles a field of rape flared yellow in the sunlight. Pulling clear of a bend he saw a chapel up ahead. He stopped the car outside the gate and walked around the squat building, the tilting gravestones.

Flowers twitched by the old walls. Brown earth, the petals, purple and blue, moving in the wind. Walker pulled open the door and stepped into the hymn-book mustiness of the church. Rows of benches, an eagle lectern, organ pipes. A stained-glass window threw a blur of colour in the middle of the aisle, highlighting the V-patterned dustprint of a shoe.

The sun had passed behind a cloud and when he stepped outside it was cool and dull. He took the wedding photo from his pocket and positioned himself where, he guessed, the photographer must have stood. The stonework around the entrance, the hinges on the door, even the gangling arm of a rose bush—all these details matched.

He climbed back in the car, tapping the steering wheel with one hand, fingering his earlobe with the other. He pulled out a map and studied possible routes, saw how close he was to the map's eastern border, twisted the key in the ignition and drove. In an hour he had passed beyond the edge of the map.

Slowly the landscape changed, becoming drier, less fertile, empty. He stopped at every gas station and asked about Carver. Twice in the next twenty-four hours he was told that a man exactly answering his description had bought gas a couple of days earlier. Driving a blue Olds, travelling with two other men.

'Any idea where they were heading?'

'Only one way they can head,' said the pump attendant, wiping a sleeve across his forehead and pointing east.

He continued driving, the landscape reducing itself to nothing, a flatness that existed only to have a road built through it. He passed through a region devastated by shelling. All around were bomb craters, rusting shell cases, burnt-out vehicles. Desert suggested the denudation of a landscape to a state of nothingness, but here the desert had been pulverized into something else, less than desert. Bombs had blown the desert apart but, since there was nothing to be blown apart, what remained was ruined emptiness.

Later he saw a yellow smudge over the horizon: a town. He drove past white houses and the entrances of large woody drives and private roads. In the city itself orange trees and palms lined litterless roads. He pulled over at a bar with tables outside. A few people were reading papers, people who didn't need jobs. There was an identical bar across the road. The menu listed dozens of different juices, lush combinations of exotic fruit, each so delicious that it took a massive exertion of will not to drain the glass in two seconds flat—and even then you ended up downing it in under ten.

'What's the name of this town?' he asked the waitress who was slim and gorgeous.

'Juice Town,' she said, smiling and scooping up a tip from the table next to him.

It was a good name. Everyone drank juices and ate perfect fruit and was tanned and thin and fit—except for those who worked out at the fruit-processing plant. For them life was hell. They hated the sight of mangoes, kiwis, and kumquats and spent their time getting wasted on cheap beer in the dangerous bars of the city's south side.

The waitress—her name was Nadine—told him all this when he ordered his second juice cocktail. He had driven into Juice

Town through the white suburbs and would be leaving through the sprawling black ghetto. It wasn't safe to drive there after dark; it was best to stay the night and head off first thing in the morning. He could stay at her place, she said. If he wanted to.

Her shift finished two hours later. Walker drove, Nadine gave directions. She was studying architecture and her apartment was cluttered with records, catalogues, and a large drawing board. Sketches lay flattened on the drawing board or curled up on the floor around it. Nadine singled out a few for Walker's inspection and then wandered off. They were studies of gargoyles with rabid teeth and bulging eyes, peering through a sleet of charcoal. While Walker was looking through them she called from the bedroom to put on a record. The sound of the shower came on.

Her albums were scattered over the floor. As he picked through them he realized he had never seen any of the things Rachel owned: her books, her tapes, useless things she had bought on holiday. Only a few of her clothes.

Walker put on the record that was on the turntable, an Indian singer called Ramamani whose name meant nothing to him. Her voice filled the room like all the happiness and all the forgiveness there could ever be.

Nadine emerged a few minutes later, wrapped in a towel, her hair streaming wet. He kissed her on the neck and she let the towel drop to the floor.

He left early, in the grey half-light. He spent his life leaving. The idea of home, for Walker, had always lain perpetually in the future. That was what had made prison bearable for him, the indefinite deferment of the present. Waiting for his life, for the consequences of his actions, to begin or to end, whichever it was.

None of the juice bars were open yet. The streets got gradually worse, the houses more decrepit. The only places open were grim twenty-four-hour cafés. Houses gave way to shacks and where before phone lines had connected smart apartment blocks to each other, here washing lines linked each shack to the next. The road became more potholed until it abandoned any claims to being a surfaced road and resigned itself to being a dry brown track the width of a freeway.

The sun had struggled over the blue mountains in the distance, made even more beautiful by the misery they looked down on. To the right was the giant fruit-processing plant. It sprawled for miles, like a city in its own right. The road curved towards it and then pulled away again. Walker's side of the road was practically empty but as he left the fruit factory behind the traffic coming towards him swelled in volume. Cars and buses, men walking in the cold dawn of a hot day. At a set of lights he waited nervously as a thin gang of youths stared from a sidewalk corner. He gripped the wheel, expecting a rock to come crashing through his windshield. Then the lights changed and he moved on.

There seemed no end to the ghetto and the further he went the worse the housing became. Soon there weren't even shacks, just lengths of corrugated iron or plastic sheets lashed together to provide a notion of shelter. It got worse and worse and then— although it didn't get any better—it got less and less until, with the sun easing itself into the morning, he found himself surrounded by scrubland. Even this scrubland was touched by the misery which each year intruded further into it but then the clumps of burnt cans and dismal plants gave way to the flat expanse of desert, the simple angles of sun and sky.

It grew warm; he wound down the window, propped his arm on the door.

Early afternoon, the road forked. No sign. Walker stopped the car and got out. Both options were identical. The surrounding silence was immense and empty. He crouched down and tried to decipher the crisscrossed traces of tyre patterns. Kicked by a breeze, a faded Coke tin rattled across the ground. Standing up again he could see the residue of marks curving off to the left. He returned to the car and moved off, adding tracks of his own, leaving them.

He had driven for sixty featureless miles when he passed a sign warning of road works. As he drew closer he saw that the work was being done by a chain gang. Rifles, guards, the sullen rhythm of picks and spades. The real purpose of a chain gang, Walker saw now, was to serve as a warning to any potential felon who happened to drive past. Pairs of eyes turned towards him as he slowed and stopped. Nothing else changing, only the tension spreading like sweat. As soon as he opened the door a guard cocked his rifle and aimed it straight at Walker's face. The sound of shovels and picks died away until a guard gestured to the men to keep working. The air was brittle with hate and fear. The guards wore aviator shades. Walker's reflection ricocheted from one pair to another. He raised his hands high. The glasses of the guard nearest him showed the horizon. Desert and sky, no room for anything between them, not cruelty even or punishment.

'I wanted to . . .' Surprised at the dryness of his mouth, he cleared his throat and began again. 'I just wanted to know what the next town up the road is.'

The gang had stopped working again and this time the guards did nothing about it. All eyes were turned on Walker. He heard gum being chewed. Sweat dripped and sizzled on the parched ground. The sun throbbed in his eyes.

'The next town,' he repeated.

'Next town is Sweetwater,' said the guard nearest him.

'Also, I wanted to know if a blue Olds had passed this way in the last couple of days.'

'Back in the car,' the guard said, knowing his power was diminished by words.

'I just—'

'Back in the car.'

Walker nodded and turned around, hands still raised. As he made his way to the car one of the prisoners caught his eye and nodded, yes.

SWEETWATER WAS SUCH A DISMAL TOWN THAT WALKER DECIDED to press on to Eagle City. It was a long haul and by the outskirts of Attica, a vast sprawling city, barely a hundred miles from Sweetwater, both Walker and the car were coming apart under the strain. Second gear was only intermittently available; fourth had given up completely so he whined along in third, keeping to sixty despite the roar of complaints from the engine. Walker was exhausted. He missed the turn off for the Attica orbital and was being sucked into the city. One highway fed into another until he found himself on a six-lane freeway that curved and arched, dipped over other larger freeways. The volume of traffic, the speed, and the size of the roads, all filled him with a surge of indifferent excitement: just keeping up with the flow of traffic made you feel like you were racing ahead. Cars slipped back and forth between lanes, moving over all six lanes in the space of half a mile and then making their way back. The road signs—bright blue, huge white letters inscribed on an enamel sky—showed no destinations, only the names of other smaller or larger freeways which in turn led to other freeways. To Walker, frazzled by tiredness, caught up in this relentless flow, the idea of houses began to seem quaint, ridiculous. He passed over another coil of roads and felt as if he and the other drivers were electrons in a huge laboratory model, flying particles of energy. Arrival or departure meant nothing, all that mattered was to keep hurtling along with everyone else. Even the idea of pulling off for gas contradicted the fundamental principle at work here: keep moving.

The freeway had now increased to eight lanes which were splitting in two like a long grey zipper coming undone. Walker kept his foot planted to the floor and pulled away to the left, the car shaking and buffeting around him. Soon the freeway fed into another even faster one. Cars swerved and slalomed across the road. Ten lanes of traffic howled and roared along.

Initially Walker had intended keeping to the left, but two and then three lanes of traffic had somehow squeezed between him and the hard shoulder and now he was engulfed in a whitewater torrent of cars. He caught glimpses of other drivers, ashen and pale as if they had surrendered themselves to an activity over which they had no control. Nose to tail at sixty miles an hour. Walker's engine was screaming and rattling; he was sure he could smell burning. He tried fourth gear, thought for a moment he had it and then realized he was freewheeling. Tried to slip the stick back into third but third had locked like a gate. Feeling the first surges of panic he allowed the gearstick to float into the free space of neutral and then tried to ease it as gently as possible into fourth, hoping to take the gearbox by surprise. When that failed he grabbed the stick with his left hand and wrenched it hard. A shriek from the gearbox. He was losing speed. Cars were flashing lights in his mirror. He tried fourth, third again, second—nothing. As he slowed he saw angry faces in the cars lashing by his window. To stop here was a crime. It went against the fundamental reason for being on the road, contravened something so basic as to horrify and frighten those who witnessed it.

As a last attempt he switched the engine off, waited a few seconds, switched on again and tried second gear—nothing. Fourth—nothing. He was down to twenty miles an hour, three lanes from the left, four from the right, cars rushing by on either side. Only now that he was coming to a halt did he fully appreciate the speed of traffic all around. Cars were flashing blurs of metal. He flicked on the hazard lights but nothing happened: it was as if the car had experienced a massive coronary and died instantaneously. He tightened the seat belt as the car drifted to a halt. Cars were swerving to avoid him, bearing down and then indicating frantically and pulling out into another lane. He saw a truck moving towards him, heard the squeal of brakes, saw it filling the rear window. Braced himself for the impact, raised his legs clear of the steering wheel and at the last second the truck veered, screeching to the left. It was like being a coconut in a shy. All he could do was wait for the smash of impact. Huge seconds passed. Already thirty cars had zoomed by and narrowly missed. Swerving clear, a car clipped his trunk and nudged the Ford around so that it was now at a slight angle to the flow and presented a bigger target. A van grazed the back bumper and tugged Walker round until he was at right angles to the traffic. A third car ploughed into the front left fender. A rending sound of metal, a drizzle of glass and then still another crash as something thundered into the back. A blur of movement. The seat belt bit into him as the car, entangled with another, was shunted forward. He looked up and saw that the Ford had been completely turned around and was now facing into the oncoming traffic.

He flicked open his seat belt and clambered into the back. There was another crunch and the whole of the front seat was a jagged concertina of metal. The car had caved in around him as if it were being scrapped. Another vehicle piled into the one that had hit him, and then another until Walker was protected from the impact by the buffer of vehicles joining the pileup. Oil began spurting from a ruptured pipe. The smell of petrol.

By now knowledge of the crash had filtered back along the freeway, traffic all around had come to a halt. There was hardly room for Walker to move but he was unhurt. He looked through the spiderweb cracks of the window and saw a snake of petrol coiling around the car. The door was jammed but one kick and the window disappeared. He clambered through the gap, the wail of sirens already approaching.

Four or five cars were tangled together. A young woman pulled herself clear of her wrecked car. Together she and Walker checked the other drivers. Two were trapped in the wreckage of their cars but even they shouted with shocked exuberance that they were OK, they were OK.

Cops arrived. Nobody was sure what had happened. There was talk of a car breaking down, stalling. Walker joined in, explaining he had slowed to avoid a car in front of him that had practically stopped in the middle of the highway.

Patrol cars and ambulances kept arriving. The wreckage was slashed by blue lights. Walker grabbed his holdall from the back seat and limped—despite an abundance of stretchers—to an ambulance which began squeezing its way along the hard shoulder.

At the hospital the sense of unity which bound together the survivors of the crash was dispersed among the chaos of pain and injury that waited and hurried all around. Cops and hospital staff began taking details of who was driving which vehicle, trying to discover exactly what had happened. Knowing that he couldn't explain how he came by his car, Walker took advantage of the white bustle of activity to move away in the direction of the toilets. Once out of sight he ducked down another corridor and disappeared into a labyrinth of wards and specialist departments. It was a large hospital and when he emerged from the lemon-scented fluorescence it was into a tree-lined street that contrasted sharply with the swarming forecourt where the ambulances arrived.

He had ended up in Attica literally by accident and wanted to get out of town as quickly as possible. He flagged down a cab which took him to the bus terminal. The bus to Eagle City had already left so he bought a ticket as far as Odessa. He was so tired it took an effort of will just to make his way to his seat. Getting out of Attica, negotiating the tangled ribbon of freeways would take hours. It didn't matter. By the time the bus pulled clear of the terminal he was asleep.

He was shaken awake by the driver saying, 'We're here, buddy.'

'Where's here?' Walker had slept so deeply it took him a few moments to remember he was on a coach. His knee ached, memories, dreams, thoughts began to untangle.

'Odessa,' said the driver.

'And what time is it?'

'Time for breakfast, buddy. You look like you could use some.'

Walker limped along the aisle after the driver, stepped down into the blue hunger of morning. He walked through a diner and dunked his head under the washroom tap. His face was there waiting in the mirror when he looked up.

He ordered coffee, cereal, pancakes, eggs, more coffee. Sitting a couple of places along the counter was a red-faced guy, wading through a breakfast of comparable size. Nodded at Walker between chews.

'Some breakfast, ain't it?'

Walker nodded back, holding up his fork to indicate his mouth was too full to speak.

'Just off the bus?'

'Yeah. From Attica.'

'Where you heading?'

'Eagle City. You know about buses there?'

'There's one late this afternoon. Used to be one in the morning as well but they stopped that.'

They went back to eating, ordered more coffee. The guy was called Ray and he was on his way to Crowville. He had a few things to do first here in Odessa, he said, but Walker could come with him as far as Crowville halfway to Eagle City. From there he could get a train or a bus easy. Walker agreed immediately and they shook hands as if clinching a deal.

An hour later they were sitting in the front of Ray's pick-up, nosing their way out of town. For the first twenty miles they chatted and then fell into an easy silence, broken only when one of them said 'Look' and pointed to a black flop of buzzards up ahead, a rabbit streaking across the highway. They had been travelling for just over two hours when Ray got a call on short-wave telling him he had to go to New Bedford, a hundred miles away to the north, to pick up a crate of spares. Urgent. There was a brief argument and then Ray hung up.

'Shit.'

'It's no problem,' said Walker. 'I can hitch.' There was little traffic but anyone who passed by would pick him up.

'I've got a better idea,' said Ray.

They continued for ten minutes and then turned down an unsurfaced road, little more than a track, the kind of road you drove down when you wanted to dispose of a body. After a couple of miles he stopped and they both got out of the car.

Warm, blue skies, only a breeze moving. Ray pointed off into the distance and said, 'Walk due south, where I'm pointing. After an hour, hour and a half, you'll come to some railroad tracks. I'd take you myself but the terrain's too rough for the pick-up. Follow the track west and you'll see it start climbing. After about half an hour the gradient is enough to slow the freights right down. You can hop one no problem. It's a busy piece of track. Anything going west will be heading to Eagle City.'

Walker nodded and looked in the direction indicated. Ray hunted around in the back of the pick-up and handed him a gallon container of water, a bottle of Pepsi, bread, fruit, biscuits. Walker stuffed everything except the water into his rucksack and slipped his arms through the straps. He was touched by Ray's efficient concern and when they shook hands and said good-bye he felt like he was parting from a friend he had known for ten years.

'Don't forget,' said Ray as he climbed back in the car. 'Head straight south. It won't matter if you veer a bit to one side—it'll just mean a longer or shorter walk once you hit the rails.'

With that he twisted the key in the ignition and turned the pick-up round. Waved and headed back up the road, leaving Walker in the dust-settling emptiness.

After walking for half an hour the landscape became fertile and wild, twitching with butterflies. He passed through knee-length grass and a field so dense with strawberries that their juice stained his shoes. Buffalo clouds roamed the sky. Then, in the distance, he saw the river-glint of the railroad tracks and quickened his pace, smiling.

When he got to the railroad he looked back at the wavering

track he had cut through the grass and began following the rails west, the gradient steepening all the time. After a couple of miles he stretched out by them and waited for the train, drowsy from the walk and heat. He shaded his face with a shirt and dozed.

He woke and gulped some water, ate the last of the strawberries he had picked on the way. The light was softening, his shadow reaching out along the track. Three geese angled towards the horizon: everything straining into the distance.

Waiting.

It was almost sundown when the rails began to sing. The noise got louder and soon he could see the train pulling slowly towards him.

The train was so long that three minutes after the engine had passed there was still no sign of the rear coach. Then, seeing an open boxcar approaching, he ran alongside, tossing in his bag. The length of the train made its speed deceptive. He had to sprint to keep up with the boxcar and when he reached up to haul himself aboard the momentum jolted his arms and tugged him off his feet. Dangling from the train he touched the ground again before swinging his feet up and into the car.

Once it had pulled up the incline the train began moving faster. Hanging slightly from the door he could see the long line of freights stretching away in both directions as the rails began curving slightly to the south. Mostly, he lay on the jolting floor, head propped on his rucksack, watching the sun smoulder over the horizon and the fields blazing fire-red. For a while the sky was streaked with purple and then, as the blue blackened, the first stars blinked on.

It was a warm night. He sipped water and chewed hunks

of bread, wished he had saved some of the strawberries. Later the momentum of the train lulled him to sleep. He dreamed of Rachel doing ordinary things, things he had never seen: cleaning her teeth, deciding which clothes to wear, reading, drying herself after a bath. He dreamed of her sleeping, dreaming of him.

Throughout the night he woke uncomfortably on the hard boards, looked out at the star-clogged sky until the clack of wheels tugged him asleep again.

BY MORNING THE TRAIN WAS PASSING THROUGH A SILENT EXPANSE of wheat. When the sun moved over the roof and slid in through the open door Walker retreated to the back of the car, into the cool. From here, with the golden fields and blue sky framed by the black doors, the view was exactly like the projected image of a movie screen, an endless panning shot of prairie.

Then, slowly, the view began to shrink. Houses began to appear, roads; in the distance, factories. By late afternoon the train was heaving into the outskirts of Eagle City. The number of tracks visible from the freight increased until they stretched away like a wide river.

Walker's train clanked and squealed over points, drawing parallel to other trains and then sliding away again. Beyond the railroad tracks was an actual river. A bridge squatted iron-heavy in the distance. Cranes, warehouses, water towers, and brooding clouds. Faded signs with speed limits and warnings that no longer mattered. Old stock that had been plundered for spares and left to rust in sidings. The broken windows of an abandoned signal house. Littered with gulls, even the sky looked old, run-down.

The train slowed almost to a crawl. Walker jumped down and waited for it to pass, guessing that the centre of the town was on the other side, away from the river. Some way off a gang of workers in orange bibs walked across the tracks, shovels and picks over their shoulders.

When the train had passed, Walker began making his way across the expanse of tracks, ducking under the bumpers of stationary coaches, stepping ahead of departing freights. Beyond the station rose the office blocks of the city's business district, high glass buildings made from cubes of sky.

Next to the railroad was a car park, cordoned off by a high perimeter fence. Walker waited behind a stationary shunter until there was no one in sight and then tossed over his bag and hauled himself up, the fence sagging and bulging with his weight. He dropped to the other side and walked out of the car park and into the town.

Eagle City had grown up as a crossing point and small port on the Eagle River; with the coming of the railroads it became the commercial centre of the region and was now a large, depressed town on the edge of the prairie. Walker spent two days asking after Malory or Carver without success. He had lost track of them both. Which meant that he himself was lost. He thought about leaving and going on to Despond, a couple of hundred miles away, but did not have the confidence to rationalize this in his usual way: if *he* felt like leaving, then the chances were that Malory had felt the same. Besides, what would he find there? Sitting on the steps of an abandoned building, drinking milk from a bottle, he glanced up and saw, on the wall opposite, a torn poster for a Western. In films cowboys spoke of the trail going cold, but he had no way of knowing if the trail had gone cold or had actually frozen over. And what trail was there except the one that he left in his wake? What else was there to guide him?

He tossed the empty milk bottle into a bin and began walking. Soon after embarking on the search he had given up trying to guess the real significance of what Rachel had asked him to do. He had concentrated instead on the smallest things, on a trail of imagined footprints. He had given no thought to where they might ultimately lead because the question overwhelmed him, dwarfed his efforts and made them seem futile, absurd—whatever that meant. Now that he was pondering the larger purpose of the search he felt, for the first time, like giving up, abandoning it. And then what? Abandoning things was all very well but what did you do once you had abandoned them? Something else. It was impossible to walk out on one thing without walking into another . . . What Rachel had asked him to do. Perhaps it was as simple as that. He had left so that he could return. All this shit just so he could fuck her. Like a story he'd heard in prison, using up the nothing days.

He had come to a network of steam-drift streets, crowded with cafés, bars, and clubs. He walked past a club where a new kind of music was playing loudly. A bottle smashed a few yards in front of him. Whoops of laughter and a voice calling out: 'Sorry, man, just an accident.' Walker looked up to a second-floor balcony: a guy with his arms around a giggling woman, the pair of them so huge it seemed likely that the next thing to come down would be the balcony itself. 'Take a full one with my apologies,' he said, letting a beer bottle drop from his hand. Walker caught it, twisted off the top and took a gulp, held it up appreciatively. He smiled and walked on, pleased with himself for catching the bottle, ears ringing with the laughter of the pair on the balcony.

Pounding from the entrances to clubs, different kinds of music thumped together in a disjointed beat. The streets were littered with vomit, glass, even, Walker realized with revulsion, a bloody clump of teeth. A drunk lurched towards him, his face reeling yellow and blue in the flash of lights. His hands were on Walker's lapels. Walker began pushing him away but already his battered mouth was spraying words: 'He's in Despond. That's where you'll find him. He's waiting for you.'

From across the street a guy came crashing through the window of a bar. The shower of glass held a thousand scattered glimpses of the scene before falling like hail over the figure sprawled on the sidewalk, blood laking around him. The drunk had let go of Walker, had vanished in the booze-sodden crowd. Walker looked round, could see no sign of him. There was a cheer from the bar and then silence, passersby standing clear as the guy on the sidewalk dragged himself to his knees, shambled to his feet. He swayed uncertainly, gazing into the bar until a stool came spinning through the window and knocked him back into the angled grit of glass. Another cheer from the bar. This time he didn't have the strength to get to his feet and he crawled away from the window on his hands and knees. Another stool came sailing out, followed by a chair, glasses and more stools, the remains of the window. The man sagged under the bombardment and lay motionless, one arm curled protectively around his head, surrounded by a broken mass of furniture. A dapper man from the bar stepped through the window frame and stood over him, counting him out—one-ah, two-ah—all the way to ten until he waved his arms to declare the bout over and stepped back through the window. All around from the street and bar were whoops, cheers, and applause until people drifted away.

Walker moved on, replaying the drunk's few words over and

over. The crowds thinned out. He came to the river and gazed across at an area of derelict buildings. The girders and pillars of burnt-out tower blocks showed stark against the sunset. Something in the nature of skyscrapers suggested that these bare skeletons of metal represented the final flourishing of their vertiginous aspiration: this is how they had been intended to look.

The river was dappled red by the sun as Walker made his way along the towpath. Further along the path was barricaded off and he entered the fringes of the Latin Quarter. Lines of washing hung between cramped balconies, the late silhouettes of birds were hemmed in by the redness of the sky. Preoccupied with the drunk's startling appearance Walker had been paying little attention to exactly where he was. He had been told to be careful in certain parts of the Quarter at night and became abruptly anxious. A pair of youths in ripped jeans and biker jackets appeared from around a corner, nodded as they passed by.

Top-floor windows glowed furnace-red but it was growing dark in the narrow streets. Walker glanced round and in the shadows behind him thought he detected a figure moving. When he looked again there was nothing. Dogs barked nearby. From behind, car headlights illuminated the street and flung his shadow up the wall of a building to his right. He turned down a one-way street and stepped into shadows. The car slowed by the NO ENTRY sign then continued on its way, perpendicular to the street Walker was now on.

He walked for a few blocks, past a grocery store—closed now—whose name he recognized from earlier on. If he was right, then Canal Street, at the edge of the Quarter, was only five minutes away—though in which direction he was not sure. A car slowed to let him cross the road. He gestured 'thanks' and stepped out from the sidewalk, trying to see the driver behind the dark windows.

The car turned the corner after him. He trotted across the road, walked briskly to the next right. The instant he was out of sight of the car he sprinted thirty yards, hoping that by the time it turned the corner he would have disappeared around another. When headlights swept the walls and filled the street he resumed walking. Up ahead was another one-way street. He trotted as soon as he was round the corner and was relieved to see that the car did not follow him. In evading the car, though, he had lost all sense of direction. He didn't even know the name of the street he was in, the area was totally deserted: no cars, no shops, no passersby. He wondered if the driver had been deliberately nudging him in this direction so as to intercept him a few blocks later. He looked up and down the street and began running back to the crossroads.

He was almost there when the street was again filled with the white lights of a car behind him. He heard the car accelerate. No longer attempting to disguise his urgency, he sprinted to the crossroads. He ran to another one-way street where a sign said CLOSED—ROADWORK and this time the car trailed him into it. The street was so narrow that there was no sidewalk, just enough room for a car. After running thirty yards he could see no side streets between himself and the roadworks.

He was trapped. He stopped running, breathing hard. The car stopped. High up in the gap between buildings was a glinting catwalk of sky. He heard the car revving behind him. Up ahead, flashing yellow lights and black-and-yellow tape indicated where the road had been dug up. He began running again, knowing he would never make it that far. The car revved harder. There was a screech of rubber and the street was filled with the roar of the car accelerating, bearing down on him. The roadworks were a hundred yards away. He stopped, turned. Began running straight at the approaching car, into the white glare of the headlights.

The car was a wall of white lights and noise. He had to wait till the last possible moment, a split second before he was splashed all over the windshield, until—

'—NOW!'

The word exploded from his throat. He leapt as high as he could, forcing himself higher, tucking his feet under his body, the bonnet rushing beneath him, the windshield and roof slipping by beneath him until something clipped his foot, destroying his balance and sending him tumbling down the sloping back of the car.

He hit the floor hard, jarring his wrists, gouging lumps out of his palms and knees—but he'd made it, he'd made it. Not even winded. He looked up at the brake lights straining red as the car ricocheted from one wall to the next, trailing sparks and ploughing into the barriers and lights of the roadworks. With flashing hazard lights sprawled all around and one wheel still spinning in midair it looked as if both car and street had been ripped apart by a land mine.

Walker was trembling, his knee was throbbing and cut, his palms bleeding. He had an impulse to sit down in the street and let someone bandage his cuts. Hauling himself to his feet took more effort than the jump. His strength had left him. He forced himself to trot to the end of the street and turn left, back the way he had come. It was only after he had put several streets between himself and the crashed car that he slowed to a walk. He was shaking so much he had to stop and rest for several minutes but, now that his panic had subsided, it proved surprisingly easy to find his way back to Canal Street. On Canal he hailed a taxi and gave the name of his hotel, clenching himself tight to control his shaking for the duration of the journey.

Seeing his ripped trousers, bloodied hands, and ashen face, the hotel desk clerk asked if he had been in an accident.

'Not quite,' he said, leaning on the lift button.

'You need first-aid box?'

'Could you bring it up?'

'*Si, si.*'

Back in his room he took off his shirt and shoes and filled a bath. His trousers were stuck to his knee, swollen, hurting. He eased himself into the stinging water and lay soaking before floating them off. There was a knock at the door—the clerk—and Walker called out to just leave the box on the bed, everything was fine, thank you.

Luxuriating in the feel of hot water over his limbs, bruised but still intact, he went over the scene again and again: the car stalking him, the white charge of headlights, the flashing reflection of the windshield, the roof sliding beneath him, almost clearing it perfectly until he clipped his toe like an athlete hitting a hurdle and falling to the road in the wake of exhaust and noise. It was amazing that he had got away so lightly: grazes, gravel in his hands, a cut knee—but nothing, nothing really . . .

He reached a hand out of the water and touched the chain Rachel had given to him. Smiling to himself, he thought of Kelly standing in the midst of devastation, naked except for the stone around his neck and his indestructible shorts.

He hauled himself out of the bath and reached for the towel. He climbed into bed, easing his knee gingerly between the sheets.

Tomorrow, first thing, he would head to Despond.

HE ARRIVED THERE AT MIDDAY, HIS KNEE STIFF AND TENDER FROM the cramped confines of the coach. It turned out to be a grim desert town lacking any distinguishing characteristics—which made it all the more puzzling that not only had Malory come here but he had spent longer here than any of the other places he had been. There was nothing to detain even the most thorough visitor, but almost everyone Walker asked had some recollection of Malory. Slightly bemused by the suggestion that he might have left town, they said he was sure to be around some place—as if he had just stepped outside to get a bite to eat and would be back in a few moments. The prospect of being so close to Malory should have excited him but Walker felt oddly deflated, as if he hardly cared.

Each night he ate at the bus station diner and then went back to his motel room and watched TV. One evening a guy gnawing ribs at the bar suggested he try a rooming house over in the east of the city—Malory was living there, last he'd heard. Walker resolved to head over there the next morning but when it came to it he could not face the prospect of the long journey across town, seizing on the dull ache in his knee as an excuse. Later that week, when he did drag himself over, nobody at the boarding house had ever heard of a guy called Malory. He hung around a few more days and decided it was pointless to spend any more time there: Malory had left, he was certain of that. Tomorrow he would do the same.

The next morning, however, he found he had no urge to leave and once again dawdled the day away. By evening he was furious with himself for having squandered yet another day and made up his mind to leave town first thing in the morning. The following day he loitered his time away until the evening when—as on each of the nights to follow—he was seized with a feverish determination to leave. His resolution was always particularly acute after a few drinks; then it seemed inconceivable that so much time had already gone by like this. What was so difficult about leaving? All he had to do was pack up his stuff and turn up at the bus station. Nothing could have been easier. Tomorrow he would leave. So intense was his desire to be up and on the move that he had trouble getting to sleep. His thoughts paced the room as he hatched wild schemes to make up for the time he had wasted in Despond. It took hours to get to sleep and by the time he woke the bus had already left. Every night he was filled with resolution and every morning he was devoid of energy. A couple of times he woke early, looked at his watch, and saw that if he got up now he could catch the bus but, on each occasion, he felt so drowsy, so worn out by his mental exertions of the night before, that he was unable to face the effort of getting out of bed into the greyish cold. Instead he turned over, loving the fart-warmth of his bed, and slept on until the sun had climbed into the lunchtime sky.

When he did get up it was with a feeling of contentment which turned to disappointment in the afternoon and which, by the evening, had mounted to a frantic urge to leave. The longer this went on the worse it became: the more urgently he wanted to leave at night the less inclined he felt to do so in the morning.

As time went by even the normal chores of the day came to seem burdensome. The more time he had the less he did with it. During his first few days in town he had done exercises but soon the thought of a sit-up exhausted him. He began to lose track of time. He no longer changed his sheets, stopped washing his clothes. For food he had relied on fruit and biscuits and all-day breakfasts at the diner, but now he dropped the fruit and made do with biscuits and breakfasts. Since he gnawed biscuits throughout the day he could see little point in cleaning his teeth. Why bother when he would be munching biscuits again in five minutes? The same with shaving: what was the point when you'd have to do it again in a day's time? Some days he lay in bed all morning, thinking how satisfying it would be to be a junkie, to have that sense of purpose each day, knowing you had to score. In another way he was glad to be spared the effort: even going to the shops was an exertion he dreaded. Sometimes he sat for upwards of an hour, needing to piss but unable to force himself out of the chair and into the dismal bathroom. He took to sleeping in the afternoons—far and away, he decided, the best part of the day. He loved waking up and—for a few moments—not knowing where or who he was. Then his head gradually enclosed itself around his thoughts and, still clinging to the fond memory of sleep, he became slowly aware of the first faint rumblings of what by the evening would be a bearable despair.

Each day the sun came up and the sky blued over and darkened again until sunrise the next day. Walker rarely thought of Malory. The whole idea of trying to find him seemed a waste of time and energy he didn't have. Besides, he realized, rummaging through his stuff one afternoon, he had lost the documents Malory was supposed to sign. Not that he cared one way or the other. And Carver? He'd probably bump into him in a bar somewhere in town. They'd get drunk together, play pool and talk about what a waste of effort it had all been.

Occasionally he picked up the Dictaphone and listened to the soundings he had taken so that the motel room was filled with the faint noise of other rooms. Several times he turned on the machine, thinking it might be worth recording his current condition. Unable to think of anything to say, he muttered, 'Fuck it,' and clicked it off. He lay where he was and pulled out the photo of Rachel. He had spent whole days like this in prison, staring at the image of a woman, numb with longing. He looked at her hair, her eyes. Reached for the phone and dialled her number. The machine did not click on. After eight rings the tone became bleak. In case she was just coming through the door he let it ring another ten times, hoping that when she got back she could tell that he had called, furniture and walls preserving his message. Then he just let it ring, the phone pressed to his head like a pistol, her picture in his hands.

Eventually even the drunken, nocturnal desire to leave began to evaporate—and this, oddly, was what prompted him to leave: the knowledge that if he stayed any longer he would never escape. He knew he would have to go tomorrow. It was his last chance. That night he had a troubled sleep, full of images of regret and things he had left behind: women, jobs, homes, things he'd never had in the first place. He woke early, the sun still struggling to clear his windowsill. The bus would arrive in thirty minutes. Everything was as he hoped—except he did not want to leave. It was not that he had no desire to leave: no, he actually wanted to stay, that was what he wanted. He liked it here, it wasn't such a bad place.

By mid-afternoon he was wretched with despair and that night he hit the bar early. He sat next to a guy who had been living in Despond for the last fifteen years. He had just been passing through but, gradually, had taken a kind of liking to the place. There were plenty worse places.

Walker bought two more beers and clunked glasses with the guy. Looking at him he understood how unhappy marriages could last tens of years, how people survived amputations and debilitating illness. He thought of rushing back to his room, packing his bag, and just walking out of town. No sooner had he formulated it than he recognized the ludicrousness of the scheme. There were weeks of desert in every direction. That was the thing about this place, it was impossible to take yourself by surprise; always you thought of an action before doing it and then, immediately, there ensued a reason for not doing it. He was distracted from this reverie by the old man nudging his arm.

'Ready for another,' he said. Walker looked at the old man, saw himself reflected in his eyes. He shook his head, slugged back the rest of his drink and left.

He needed to collect his belongings from his room but was almost frightened to set foot in there. He gathered up his things quickly but even in those few seconds he could feel the urge to lie down and sleep. What was the point in spending the night outside in the cold? He could stay here—not sleep, just sit up until daybreak. Shaking these thoughts from his head he moved into the bathroom to get the last of his belongings. Glimpsed his bearded face in the mirror, shattered it with his fist, and closed his palm around a shard until the pain cut through his lethargy.

Outside he looked up at the desert sky where the stars hung in the same places night after night. He stood at the bus stop, already chilled to the bone. A few people came out of the diner but after a while there was no more movement and the town appeared deserted except for buildings and sky. He squatted down on the sidewalk but that was too cold so he stood through the long night, too tired to move, too cold to sleep.

It took weeks to get light. First the darkness diminished, then the sky became grey and the shapes of things came alive. Trees appeared against the orange-blue light. It was no warmer but the day was finally arriving. The diner opened and he thought he would go inside for a coffee—and immediately drove the thought from his mind.

Eventually he heard the bus rumble into town, a slow curl of dust in its wake. Four people got off. He was the only person waiting to board. The driver looked at him with surprise when he asked for a ticket to wherever the bus was going.

'That'll be Bad Axe.'

'Bad Axe is perfect.'

Walker made his way to the back of the bus. There were few other passengers—a couple with rucksacks, an old Mexican woman, a man with a cane. He stretched out in the backseat, sun slanting in through one of the side windows. He wanted to sleep but wanted also to savour this view of the city which so few had shared. Most buildings were flat and pale brown, enlivened only by the neon signs of shops that paled in the gathering sunlight. He was struck by the sprawling extent of the town, by the number of homes that each year encroached a little further into the desert. He found it hard to believe that he had been there—how long? It hardly mattered—however long he had been there he was lucky it was coming to an end. Everything came down to luck. The search was a matter of luck, a test of luck—and luck was a test of character. You could gauge yourself by the quality of your luck. Luck was everything. He breathed a sigh of relief as the bus pulled past a half-built office block, a fence that would never be creosoted.

WALKER SHAVED AND CLEANED HIS TEETH IN THE STATION WASH-
rooms at Bad Axe. He felt sluggish but the lassitude that had overwhelmed him in Despond had evaporated and he was thinking
once again about the search, anxious to make up for the time he
had wasted. In the information office the word 'Horizon' came
into his mind—out of nowhere, for no reason. Spores were blown
around by the wind and plants sprang up where they happened to
settle. Maybe words and ideas were a kind of spore: they were in
the air and sometimes they settled on you. Feeling foolish he asked
the woman at the desk if there was a place called Horizon nearby.

'A bus leaves in twenty minutes,' she said, unstartled, un-
smiling.

As he paid for the ticket he told himself this decision was
based on a hunch, on intuition, but he knew this was not true.
Intuition suggested an instinctive version of thought, but really
he was proceeding by impulse, by whim, impatient to get moving again.

* * *

When he arrived there he thought it was not a city but one building in the city. Then, as he began to get a sense of the scale of the place, he realized that although there were no roads or streets, corridors and hallways served as thoroughfares, vast ballrooms as parks, rooms as houses. Here and there he found windows but all he could see from them, except for the damp courtyard many yards below, were the walls and windows of the rest of the building, the rest of the city. He opened doors which led to more rooms. Sometimes these were huge with high ceilings, empty except for a dark table, chairs, chandeliers. Other rooms were small with armchairs and a fireplace. A few were carpeted but most had floors of polished wood that clanged and echoed underfoot. When he stopped walking he heard other footsteps but, in the vast interiors and winding corridors, he wondered if these were the echoes of his own steps. He walked into a room with a great gilt-edged mirror, enormous as a painting of a battle or biblical scene. The mirror made the room unfathomably huge, empty of everything except its own reflected image and his tiny figure in one corner. From there he moved into a room with an oil painting over the fireplace. It showed a vast room, not dissimilar to many of those he had passed through. As he walked on through the city he saw more paintings, always of interiors. Whenever he came across a painting he hoped it might be a landscape but there was never a hint of the outdoors. He resisted any feeling of panic but gradually the sense of being trapped by the vastness of his surroundings began to alarm him. Generally, you were either lost in a wilderness—a desert or an ocean—or trapped in a confined space—a dungeon. Here Walker was simultaneously trapped in a dungeon and lost in the vastness of his confines. It would have been possible to climb out of a window and down one of the thin drainpipes that clung to the walls like rope but there was no point—they led only to the courtyard that was like an open-air dungeon. Leaning out of some windows and craning upwards he could see a colourless patch of sky but most did not afford even this prospect. Instead they simply opened on to another room. He could go where he pleased but wherever he went he came to more rooms. Like this one, empty except for a long conference table and thin black chairs. On the table was a decanter of red wine, glasses. The austerity and scale of the room made him feel like he had come for a meeting with an all-powerful bureaucrat. He poured a glass of wine, the slight tinkling of the glass magnified many times over by the acoustic vastness. Held the glass up to the light and watched the red liquid flare like a volcano erupting under the sea. He pulled a chair out and sipped the wine. It was inconceivable that a city like this—or building or whatever this place was—could go on for much longer. Even assuming it was the size of London he could still cross it in . . . how long? A couple of days? That was two days without food—there was water and wine, but so far he had seen nothing to eat—yet the prospect was daunting rather than frightening. The only thing to do was keep walking. On impulse, as he was leaving, he picked up the decanter of wine and hurled it at a wall. Knowing he could trash the place was somehow reassuring and a few moments later he carved his initials in a big oak table. Then, for no reason, he added FUCK OFF in jagged ugly letters. This act of childish vandalism cheered him up considerably and he walked out of the room with his hands in his pockets, smiling. Soon he felt sleepy from the wine and lay down on an embroidered sofa. It was difficult to sleep with nothing to cover him, so he yanked down one of the curtains and curled up beneath it.

He had no idea how long he slept. When he woke the window was dark as a blackboard but apart from that nothing had changed. Even so, the fact that it was night outside made him feel even more trapped in the city. He got up and resumed his journey through the rooms and stairs and corridors. In a large anteroom—the term made no sense, every room here was an anteroom—he found what appeared to be a visitors' book. It was half-full of names and signatures, the last of which was Malory's. He added his own and walked on.

He left Horizon as abruptly as he had arrived. He opened a door—identical to hundreds of others which he had opened during his stay in the city—and there, stretching ahead, was a road sloping into the distance.

He closed the door behind him and walked on, enjoying the empty air and the wind combing the roadside trees. After half an hour he came to a railway station. The train was about to leave and he made it with seconds to spare: as soon as he slammed the door behind him he heard a whistle and the train moved out.

He found an empty compartment but at the next station the door slid open and a tall man—thin, mid-thirties, hair clipped army-short at the back and sides—sat down opposite him. As soon as he had settled himself he put on a pair of tortoise-shell glasses and began reading: *Tom Jones,* a book Walker had half read so long ago he had forgotten almost everything about it—Tom was searching for his lost brother or mother or sweetheart. In any case, whoever he was looking for was really just an excuse to propel him on his adventures.

Seeing the man absorbed in his novel like that made Walker aware that he no longer read books. He noticed posters, tickets, words on scraps of paper, odd things scribbled in bus shelters or in the margins of timetables, signs glimpsed from the window of the train, but it never occurred to him to read a book. Noticing Walker looking at the book in his hand the guy smiled and said, 'Have you read it?'

'No, no,' said Walker smiling back, embarrassed. 'Sorry, I was just looking. What's it like?'

'Boring as shit,' the guy laughed before going back to his reading.

Walker sat back and shut his eyes. Opened them again briefly and looked out of the window. The usual stuff: clouds, trees, fields, power lines, sometimes a road. He slept and dreamed of a memory he had never had, of Rachel swimming in a pool and climbing out, smiling, her wet hair dripping. As she walked towards him he looked down at the trail of footprints stretching towards him from the blue pool, turning quickly to damp smudges and then dissolving away to nothing.

THE TRAIN HAD STOPPED. THE GUY READING FIELDING HAD GONE and the compartment was empty. He glanced out of the window and saw the station name, Independence. Groggy with sleep, he pulled his bag from the luggage rack and stepped down to the platform.

The station was deserted. A clock showed the time as ten past four. Siesta shadows crept into the waiting room, empty except for an old man staring at the ground. The faded letters of a hoarding for a paint company said: 'No colour loves the sun like yellow'. A station official was leaning out from a second-storey window, looking down the platform to where a woman was resting on a plinth-size suitcase.

Surprised by how quiet it was, Walker made his way down the worn steps leading out of the station. A man in a suit was halfway up, not moving, apparently pausing in mid-stride. As Walker made his way further down the stairs he saw that the man's left leg was actually poised an inch from the step, exactly as if he were frozen while racing for a train. Out by the ticket hall a heavy black woman and two children were buying tickets. A newspaper vendor was pointing out into the streets, offering directions to a man in a trilby who echoed the gesture with a furled newspaper. An old man leant on his broom.

In the street the silence was even stranger, for the scene that met his eyes was ostensibly that of a busy city—except that here, too, nothing was moving. Cars were everywhere—about to pull out from the kerb, accelerating away from green lights. A tall man was awkwardly craning his neck as he folded himself into a taxi. Moving away from the station Walker looked up the incline of Third Avenue and saw an army of pedestrians swarming towards him, immobile, not moving even a fraction of an inch. He looked around, amazed at the detail of activity that normally passed unnoticed: coins falling from pale fingers to a beggar's styrofoam cup. A labourer crouching at the knees to take the weight of a bag of cement which another man was tipping over the edge of a truck. Two men laughing together, one about to slap his knee with hilarity, the other leaning backwards, mouth open as if he had been shot. A woman gazing at herself in a small mirror, dabbing lipstick on to her mouth. A group of people clustered round a hot-dog stand, faces jutted forward to protect their shirts from the sauce that dripped almost to the ground. A smiling black girl reaching over to clean the windshield of a car waiting at the lights, the wipers flicked out like antennae, detergent bubbles foaming over the hood.

Walker moved between the cars, immobile but still animated by an inherent sense of speed, an invisible equivalent of the motion lines of a comic book, the slight ghosting of a photograph. He looked closely but could not see how this effect came about. With people it was easy—in every gesture you sensed the muscles straining in legs and arms—but cars looked exactly the same whether moving or stationary. Perhaps, since a car was designed to move, a sense of speed was implicit in the very idea of a car. A car in motion was simply a car; a car parked wasn't a car, it was a parked car. Hence, thought Walker, smiling at the force and speed of his logic, the sense of momentum that animated the cars frozen in the street around him. He peered into the back window of a cab, one of the passengers pressed against the door, the other leaning heavily on him as the cab took a corner.

Frozen like this every gesture had a certain perfection, each moment of a person's day—however insignificant—was worthy of the consideration you would give to a great work of art. More so in fact, for here every nuance of experience was revealed: over there a couple embracing, a woman handing coins to a flower vendor, her fingers almost touching his palm; people smiling and saying 'please' or waving 'hello'; two people who had just bumped into each other, a look of startled apology spreading over their faces.

Walker had no idea what had happened—the city reminded him of Pompeii where people were frozen in the defensive attitudes they assumed when lava poured over the ancient city—but here there was no sense of calamity: everything had just stopped. Despite this, danger was everywhere. A woman walking up a flight of stairs, a cyclist leaning hard into a curve—actions like these required a hundred acts of gymnastic balance and judgement. The sight of a waiter paused in the act of threading his way between the tables of a kerbside café, a tray of food balanced in one hand, was suffused with a suspense that was all but unendurable. Every act was potentially catastrophic. Stepping off a kerb or bending to tie a shoelace, these were actions whose outcome was not certain: it was impossible to know the consequences of anything. Every action was poised on the brink of a precipice; any moment or action brought you to the edge of infinity.

This feeling was brought home to him horribly a few blocks

further on, outside a church in Jackson Square. The police had cordoned off the area and a large crowd had gathered, their eyes fixed on something going on several yards above their heads. As Walker drew near he saw an expression of horror on many of the onlookers' faces. Some had turned away, were covering their faces with their hands. Silent though it was, a gasp of shock pervaded the whole scene. As soon as he came round the side of the church he saw why. A man had jumped from the bell tower where the arms of police and firemen reached out to restrain him. Six yards from the ground the desperate figure was frozen in his fall, a split second from the impact of his death. His jacket billowed, his hair streamed above him, his glasses, torn from his face by the speed of the fall, were suspended a foot above his head. One hand was thrust out reflexively to break his fall, to cushion the impact which perhaps would never come. Walker moved through the shocked crowd and stood directly beneath the falling figure, transfixed and horrified by what he saw. Then, fearful that time would move on again and he would be crushed, he walked quickly away from the church.

He wandered through the city in a daze, half expecting at any moment to find that his own movements were beginning to slur to a standstill. He glanced at a clock and saw the time: almost ten past four. That was when the city had stopped. Knowing this told him nothing. It could have been any time. Establishing when a given event occurred—a murder or a break-in—was normally a major step forward in solving a mystery but here it revealed nothing. It constituted the mystery rather than explained it.

He came to a corner diner and stepped inside. The Naugahyde seats held patches of sunlight, the windows merged dim reflections of the scene inside with the cars out in the street. Because it was the middle of the afternoon the diner was almost empty.

A lone drinker sat at the bar, watched by the bartend, wiping glasses. A couple of people sat at tables on their own, one of them reading a paper. Loneliness pervaded the place. Over by a window a waiter had just poured a cup of coffee for a man eating an omelette, knife raised as if to say 'when'. Walker helped himself to the coffee and sat down opposite the omelette eater. He looked closely at the man, knife and fork in hand, about to start his meal. He had a look of virtual despair—but despair stripped of desperation. In an instant it would fade to the methodical resignation of men who eat meals alone, but preserved here was a look of near-desolation that passed unnoticed in the normal flow of action.

Walker dawdled, when he left the diner, mesmerized by the complexity and abundance of activity suspended, silent as a photograph, around him. There was no narrative here—or there was a new kind of narrative, one that ran across time rather than through it. We seek explanation in terms of causality, in terms of one event succeeding another. Here simultaneity, the way every action and person in the city was linked to every other, was the only explanation. Either there was no such thing as coincidence or—and it amounted to the same thing—there was only coincidence.

Tired suddenly, Walker crossed over to the Metropolitan Hotel. In the silent bustle of the lobby he helped himself to the key to a room on the top floor. The curtains were drawn in his room and he felt relieved by the comforting dimness. He showered and climbed between the white right-angles of sheets.

He felt sure that he was getting nearer to Malory—but it was just as likely that he was further away than ever. He had no way of knowing. There was no longer any correlation between time and distance; each meant nothing in terms of the other. Perhaps Malory was a week ahead, or a day, or perhaps he was months or a year away by now. He could have been a mile away or he could have been a hundred, a thousand miles away . . . Maybe the search would never end and he would continue hunting for Malory until he was an old man, until he died. Unable to move, penniless, reduced to scanning the articles in archives. Tolerated and mocked by the library staff, perhaps managing to persuade a young enthusiast of the importance of his work, bequeathing him a deranged mass of notes, leaving future generations to complete the task to which he had dedicated his life.

He thought of people who spent their lives tracking down the Abominable Snowman or the Loch Ness Monster. The whole point of these things was that they existed only in sightings. You could never get scientific proof of their existence. That was their purpose: they were a lure, a metaphor for the Himalayas of the unknown. As soon as the Yeti was sighted it would cease to exist. 'Yeti' was probably Tibetan for a being whose existence is constantly hinted at—footprints, droppings—but cannot be proved . . . He was drifting on the edge of sleep, his thoughts becoming flecked with dreams. Time and distance. Footprints in water. Traces of dream . . .

THE CLOCK NEXT TO HIS BED WAS STILL SHOWING 4.09 WHEN HE woke. Drawing back the curtain he found the city still flooded with afternoon sunshine. Outside his window a bird was frozen in flight, wind ruffling its feathers, wings arched perfectly, eyes full of sky. He looked down into the street, the immobile crowds still there.

He took food from the kitchen and left the hotel. Nothing had changed but his internal rhythm insisted that it was morning: the streets seemed infused with the energetic bustle of people commencing their days. As he moved through the living statues he again became absorbed in the wealth of detail revealed around him. He saw a Coke can poised in midair between a cyclist's hand and the waiting bin. Across the way a workman was leaning over a pneumatic drill, another watching him, tilting back his yellow safety helmet.

In a shop window Walker saw his reflection shimmer through racks of camera equipment. He wanted to head out of town, to move on, but it was difficult to know how. There were plenty of cars but with the traffic gridlocked in time it would be impossible to move.

He continued walking until he came across a guy locking his bike to a sign. Walker extricated the bike and cycled through the city, cutting across a park where people were frozen in the act of jogging or chasing after balls, staring up at a blue disc of frisbee. A dog was leaping to catch a ball between its teeth and the trees waited for the wind to pass through their leaves. On the far side of the park there were fewer people and Walker moved more quickly towards the outskirts of the city where old people waited at bus stops and mothers pushed prams. He gave no thought to where he was heading. Motives and purpose had dissolved within him. He cast no shadow.

After cycling for an hour he had still seen no movement—no cars, no people. He crossed a bridge and cycled through a landscape of gentle hills and tree-shaped trees. A sign said CRESCENT CITY 25 MILES. He became aware of a breeze, a few clouds. A flock of birds, drifting smoke. A car came roaring towards him, passed in a swirl of grit and fumes. He saw a dog padding along the roadside, tail wagging. Minutes later he waved at a woman and a child who smiled and waved back. Their gestures—and especially the child's red bobble hat—were surprisingly familiar and as he cycled towards Crescent City little details of the landscape also touched elusive chords in his memory.

In the city itself he was constantly assailed by a sense of déjà vu. Although he had never been here before every street corner and house was steeped in memories. Entering the bakery, asking for croissants, handing over coins, the way the assistant smiled and said, *'Merci, au revoir'*—each gesture was like an echo of one that had already occurred. When the desk clerk showed him to his room at a boarding house he knew, fractionally before the door was opened, how it would be arranged: the bed tucked into an alcove, a porcelain jug and bowl on a chest of drawers, sunlight pouring into the dim room when the shutters were opened. In the days that followed a single detail often brought back a whole sequence of events: seeing two birds perched on a phone line recalled a previous time when he had walked down exactly this street, at precisely this time of the evening, with the elderly couple limping towards him.

And then there were the wind chimes which hung from the balconies of houses. All over the city the air was full of the sound of fragile tinkling. It was a beautiful sound and Walker was startled by how deeply these chimes affected him. The breeze connected houses to each other like phone lines, brushing one set of chimes fractionally before another as it made its way through the streets.

More than anything else it was these chimes that filled him with déjà vu. Each chime was less like the actual noise of the metal tubes touching than the memory of that moment, of that sound, endlessly renewed. He made a recording of the chimes but the tape made them sound like wire hangers jangling in a wardrobe, preserving none of their resonance.

The chimes haunted Walker, convincing him that he had been here before, but however hard he tried—in fact the harder he tried the more elusive the sense became—he was unable to fathom the origin of this sensation. Perhaps it was experienced by everyone who came here and the tingle of déjà vu—there was something familiar even about this sequence of reasoning— was the city's distinguishing feature, like the canals of Venice, the garbage dumps of Leonia, or the spires of Christminster. Walker's sense of following in his own footsteps grew steadily but no less subtly stronger.

Then, as he walked down Esplanade, each step adding to—without confirming—the feeling that he had done this before, he began to wonder if there were some way in which he could use this to his advantage. Until now he had been dragging memories in his wake; he had to try to allow these hinted memories to lead him onwards, to show him what to do next. Since it became more difficult to pin down the feeling the harder he concentrated, he had to make his mind blank, to cease being an active agent of his own intentions and allow the sensation to ebb and flow as he wandered. The problem was that a sense of déjà vu pervaded the entire city and as time passed the hinted memories he sought to follow became overlaid by the actual memories of the previous days. The strongest, deepest, most allusive sensations were the most elusive and least immediate.

He drifted through the city, tugged by shifting currents of memory, until he found himself outside an old wooden house, painted white. Windows, open shutters. Chimes hanging from the balcony, stroked by a breeze no longer there.

He unlatched the wrought-iron gate and walked round the side of the house. Strewn with leaves, a lawn extended from a conservatory to some flower beds, bare except for clipped rose bushes. Beyond the flower beds was a patch of rough ground and a grey-haired man scooping up armfuls of leaves and tossing them on to a bonfire. Walker stood in the middle of the lawn watching him. He appeared lost in thought, pausing in his work and watching the flames, tugging at his right earlobe with thumb and forefinger. Thin smoke smudged the sky. The man turned and looked at him, hesitated, and then resumed his work.

Repeating a sequence of events enacted before, Walker passed through the conservatory and into the house. From a ground-floor room he heard a crackly recording of a cello, a woman humming gently in tune with it, the rattle of teacups. He went upstairs and into a small study. Typed pages were scattered over the floor. He looked out of the window and saw an old woman carrying a tray of cups and plates over to a weather-worn table in the garden. The man looked up, saw her, smiled.

Beneath the window was an open rolltop desk. Propped on one side of the desk was an old postcard showing a silent piazza, empty except for a statue and striding shadows. On the back, in his own handwriting, was the name of the city in the picture: Imbria.

HE TRAVELLED THERE THE NEXT DAY. IT WAS A CITY OF EMPTY piazzas, red towers, and the endless perfect arches of arcades. Mustard-coloured walls, ochre streets. He noticed red towers and arcades but mainly he was aware of the space between things, as if there were more space here than was possible. There was no distance or direction, only perspective and white walls, mustard-coloured streets. The city looked the same in every direction—arcades, piazzas, towers, long shadows—but each new view was unfamiliar, strange. Whenever he turned a corner a new but identical vista of arcades and towers opened up before him. Only one sense mattered here. Everything was arranged for the eye.

The sky was turquoise, becoming lighter, greener, close to the pencil-line horizon. The light made the walls of the buildings glow amber. On the other side of the square was the city hall, a tower and clock face that told nothing. Time slid across the piazza in angular shadows. Always it was the shadows, dark as a girl's hair, that he noticed first. Even a stone in the middle of the piazza cast a shadow the length of a man. Shadows peeked from the edge of a wall and when he turned the corner to see what cast them his attention was held by another shadow, projected from beyond the next corner. Something seemed always to be going on just beyond the edge of his vision, around the next corner. Everything happened in the distance. In this way the city lured him through itself.

Between the mustard walls of a building he caught a glimpse of the sea. He wandered in that direction but did not get any nearer. Space swallowed him up. Shadows slid into the cool arcades. Up ahead was a red tower with flags flying. He turned a corner and there was the sea. Flat, opalescent, lapping gently beyond the low wall. Near the horizon was a triangle of sail, brilliant white. A white cane had been left propped against the wall. A statue gazed out to sea. On the seawall was a book, pages flapping in the wind—except there was no wind. Everything was still but the pages were flapping as if in a spring breeze. He moved closer to the book, listened to the rustle of the pages: as if the book were alive, like a creature whose breath had only the strength to make this faint flutter.

Out of the corner of his eye he noticed a shadow emerge from an arcade. A figure stood in the piazza where Walker himself had been standing minutes earlier. They stared at each other, each mirroring the other's reaction, neither displaying shock or alarm, and then moved on. The sky was an even deeper turquoise than before. Instead of becoming darker, the light had been squeezed, concentrated. Beyond the city was the low swell of Renaissance hills.

Walker was passing by a broken statue when, through the arches of an arcade, he saw the figure again, by the quay where he himself had been standing. Again there was a pause, a lingering surprise, and then they moved on, both looking back once. Later—

time was as difficult to judge as distance—it happened again: on this occasion the figure was standing by the broken statue.

Each time they occurred the mood of these encounters changed, imperceptibly, until they were virtually stalking each other round the city. The figure had a similar realization simultaneously, for now he looked at Walker with suspicion. Walker felt the first twinge of unease and the figure's movements immediately acquired an edge of urgency. Walker began sweating; he had an impulse to run and saw the figure trot across the piazza and disappear from sight.

He continued walking through the bewildered city, uneasy now. He glanced round and saw the figure looking at him. Walker ran across the piazza and into the darkness of an arcade. When he emerged into sunlight the figure was silhouetted, his back to Walker. Immediately, he looked around and ran off. So a pattern was established with Walker alternating between fleeing from the figure who would suddenly appear behind him and surprising this same person who would run from him.

The situation petered out exactly as it had begun. Walker felt confident he could outrace the figure who simultaneously reacted less nervously when Walker came up on him unawares. As their sense of mutual alarm diminished, so did the frequency of these encounters until they spotted each other rarely, harmlessly, at a distance, and Walker resumed his stroll through the city.

Later, lodged in the stone fingers of a statue, he found a card showing the piazza he was now walking across. He pocketed the card and walked on. At the top of a tower a flag fluttered in the absent breeze. In the distance a train steamed silently into the station. A cloud drifted over the train as if it had always been there. The light remained suspended between late afternoon and early evening, the sun never quite setting, the city receding all around.

Walker found himself once again by the quay, the sea lapping green and clear, the statue gazing calmly, the book still lying there, the cane propped by the wall. He picked up the book and leafed through it. On each page, blurred and smudged by spray from the sea, was written the name of one of the cities he had passed through, in the order he had visited them. Imbria was the second last name in the book. The last city, the only one he had not been to, was called Nemesis. Next to it, was what he assumed to be a date, 4.9.—, with the year an illegible blur of ink: five days from now.

NEMESIS WAS A MEDIEVAL TOWN BUILT ON TWO LOW HILLS, DOMIN-
ated by a vast cathedral and, for five months of the year at least,
by tourists who swarmed all over it. It was the last day of August
when Walker arrived and all the hotels and pensions were full.
After a morning's trudging he found, at an inflated price, a room
in a hotel high up on one of the hills overlooking the cathedral
and the red-tiled roofs crowding around it.

Walking through the city he became certain that the search
would end here. Maybe the trail didn't stop here but he lacked
the will to pursue it any further. In the past he had always found
something that urged him forward—or at least he had had a strong
impulse to move on. Relying on the same logic—on the same lack
of logic—that had brought him here, the fact that he had no urge
to go any further meant that the trail ended here, in Nemesis.
There had been times when he had longed for the search to be
over with but now, faced with this becoming a reality, he was
aware, sadly, of the sense of purpose it lent to everything. A bee
hovering over the petals of a flower, trees twisting in a gale, water
dripping from a faucet . . . Overlooked in the normal routine of
his life, the search filled such details with possibility. In Despond

he had almost given up and in other places he had been unsure where to go next but this was different: this time there was nowhere else to go. He had followed a trail by inventing it and now there was nothing else to follow, nothing left to invent. There was no more to discover—or what remained to be discovered would be discovered here.

He was sitting on a curved metal bench in a busy piazza: his second day in the city. He scrawled 'Imbria' on the back of the postcard he had found there and addressed it to Rachel. Picturing himself arriving back and seeing the card again made Walker think of what she had told him the night they had first met: dreaming of a garden where you pick a rose, waking to find your bed strewn with petals.

Seeing Walker seal the envelope a small boy offered to post it for him. Walker handed over a few coins and the boy ran to the other side of the piazza. Through the pigeon-scattering crowd Walker saw him stand on tiptoe and slot the card into a yellow letter box.

The man who had been sitting at the other end of the bench, meanwhile, hauled himself to his feet and left. Lodged between the metal slats where he had been sitting Walker noticed a leaflet which he picked up and read, vacantly, in the way you read nutritional information or special offers on the sides of cereal packets. It was a letter, written by a local filmmaker named Marek. He was making a film of the city and the people who visited it, the letter explained. It would be a new kind of film, made up entirely of photographs, snaps, videos and Super 8 films taken by residents or tourists who were in the city on 9 April. He would then combine the diverse material into 'a narrative montage of the city'. The success of the enterprise depended largely on the cooperation of the people themselves and he asked any visitors to send copies of the snaps or films they took that day in Nemesis. Obviously he would reinburse them for the cost of the developing. This had been made possible by the generous sponsorship of . . . Walker skimmed the list of participating film manufacturers and moved on to the bottom of the letter where he had set out the titles of his previous films, a few laudatory quotes from the press and the address to send material to.

Walker looked at the date: 9 April, the ninth of the fourth. He had assumed that the date in the book in Imbria had meant 4 September, the fourth of the ninth, three days from now; but if the dates had been set down American-style with the month preceding the day, then the date in the book was the day on which the film was being compiled.

He hurried to a pay phone, half expecting it to ring, like a dog warning him not to approach, and dialled Marek's number. Engaged. He waited a minute and dialled again. This time the phone was answered almost immediately, by the filmmaker himself. Walker explained that he was a journalist interested in Marek's work and wondered if it would be possible to do an interview. When there was silence on the other end Walker reeled off a list of the publications he wrote for, mentioned a book he was writing. Marek sounded sceptical but he agreed to meet with Walker 'for a quick chat'.

'When would be a good time?' said Walker.

'Would it be possible to come today?'

'Yes.'

'Could you come soon?'

'That would be fine.'

'In about one hour?'

'Perfect.'

Walker replaced the receiver and caught a taxi. He was full of anticipation and paid no attention to his surroundings until the cab dropped him near the docks in the warehouse district. He found the right building and jabbed the bell. The intercom cleared its throat and Marek told him to come up.

The studio was a large loft space, screened off into separate areas. Marek came to meet him and they shook hands. He was shorter than Walker, wearing an old sweater and jeans. Espresso stubble, dark eyes ringed by insomnia circles. Walker formed an impression of a man who returns from dinner at midnight, makes himself coffee, and settles down to work until dawn.

They waited for the coffee to drip and then walked to the back of the studio, to what Marek called his office. It was partitioned off from the rest of the studio and contained a desk, table, telephone, two chairs, graphics instruments. Walker set up his Dictaphone on the edge of the desk and asked Marek about his films. He had no interest, apparently, in talking about his past films but, to Walker's relief, was eager to answer questions about the new film, the city montage.

'We printed five thousand leaflets—you've seen the leaflets, yes?—in five different languages. So, twenty-five thousand leaflets. We left them in bars and restaurants, galleries. Then, from dawn of the ninth we handed them out in the main tourist parts of the city.'

As Marek talked he reached up to a shelf behind him and took down a snow-storm of the city's cathedral. He shook it up and let the snow swirl around the model's twin towers.

'We had no idea what the response was going to be. At best we expected to get, I don't know, maybe two thousand replies. There were so many things that could go wrong. You know, people just

chuck it away without reading it, others read it and aren't interested. People intend doing it but lose the leaflet or the address
or just don't get round to doing it when they get home. Or they
see their photos and think nobody could be interested in these.
It all hinged on this initial response but for a week there was
nothing. Then a few things from local people but after three
weeks it looked like it hadn't worked.'

The snow had settled, the cathedral was plainly visible. Marek
picked it up again, shook it and placed it on the table. Walker kept
glancing at the silent swirl of flakes.

'Then it started pouring in. Stuff was arriving from all over the
place, Germany, Greece, Japan, Australia. Photos were still coming in up until a month ago—by now it's just about dried up. Then
the real work had to begin. The response was almost too good.
The amount of material we had to get through was so daunting.
And that's what we've been doing for the last couple of months.'

'So what form is it taking?' asked Walker, nodding like a
journalist.

'First we needed to arrange everything in chronological order.
That's actually much easier than you think. The individual snaps
on a film are all in order and then there are other indications—
shadows, light. Sometimes there's even a clock. We've taken copies and now have everything broken down into quarters of an
hour. At the same time we've been filing everything by place, all
the shots at Piazza San Pietro, for example. That way it can all be
cross-referenced. It will make the assembling easier later on but,
you know, it's taken a lot of time and it's difficult to see the wood
for the trees.'

'You have no idea of the form it might take?'

'Some kind of form will emerge but with a mass of material like
this that doesn't happen until you start nudging it a bit. Besides,

there are all sorts of technical problems. How to integrate the snaps and the moving footage, how to get a kind of narrative.'

Marek waited for the next question; they both looked over at the snow-storm which had almost settled.

'I wonder,' said Walker, shifting in his seat. 'Perhaps it would be possible to follow an individual through the day. I mean, the person featured in one picture would crop up in the corner of another, and a third and a fourth. It might be possible to track someone's movements through the day.'

'That's something I hadn't thought of,' said Marek. 'But it might be possible, yes.' Walker could see that the idea instantly attracted Marek. He was silent and Walker sensed that he was already working through the inherent possibilities and difficulties of such a project. He picked up the snow-storm and turned it over in his hands, looked at Walker. The Dictaphone continued running, measuring the silence between the two men.

'Maybe you had this idea before you came to speak to me,' said Marek finally.

'Not exactly.'

'But you are more interested in this idea than you are in . . . What was the name of the book you are writing?'

Walker smiled, 'I am looking for a man named Malory. I believe he was in the city on 9 April, on the day of your filming.'

'That is a coincidence.'

'The more I think about that word the less sure I am of what it means. I sometimes think it means the opposite of what it's meant to,' said Walker.

'The inevitability of coincidence,' said Marek and waited for Walker to continue.

'I wonder if it would be possible to find this man in your film, to discover what his movements were.'

'It would certainly lend an element of suspense to the film.'

'Yes.'

'And what is your interest in this man?'

'That is hard to explain.'

'Has he committed some crime?'

'Not as far as I know.'

'He is not wanted by the police?'

'Possibly. No.'

'And you are not with the police?'

'No.'

'A finder?'

'No.'

'Tracker?'

'No.'

'So what are you?'

Walker shrugged.

'And you have a photo of this man?' Marek asked.

'Yes.'

'May I see it?' Walker pulled the photo out of his wallet, unfolded it and passed it over.

'Do you have any idea of what time he was at a particular place? Otherwise it is difficult to know where to start.'

Walker shook his head.

'It would be like looking for a needle in a haystack,' said Marek.

'Well, maybe not as simple as that,' said Walker.

They started their search that afternoon. Reasoning that Malory must almost certainly have passed through the Piazza de Repubblica, the main square, they went through that pile, one of the biggest, first. On the assumption that he hadn't posed for any snaps they discounted the people featured in the photographs and concentrated on figures in the margins, people who had strayed unintentionally into the picture frame.

It was painstaking, frustrating work and by two in the morning their early enthusiasm had been overwhelmed by the drudgery of unrewarded labour. They still had two-thirds of the pile to go through but decided to call a halt and resume in the morning. Marek searched around the studio for a camp bed and then they sat by the desk drinking beer. They were bleary-eyed, half-stupid with looking, so addicted to the task that, even as they spoke, they continued to pick up odd snaps, glancing at them. Walker drained the final drops from his can, picked up one last snap—and there was Malory. The picture showed a Japanese girl smiling at the camera, a handbag over one shoulder. In the foreground the photographer's shadow groped towards her. To her right a couple were sat on some steps, eating, and to her left, walking towards the camera, was Malory. Walker reached for the magnifier and immediately Malory's face, blurred and grainy, loomed into view.

'I've found him.'

Marek came round the desk and looked over Walker's shoulder. 'You're sure it's him?'

'Take a look.' Marek looked from the magnifier to the original and back again.

'We're in business,' he said and cracked open a bottle of vile-tasting spirits to celebrate. Grimacing, they took a shot each.

Within ten minutes of waking they were back in the office, swallowing dark coffee, munching croissants.

'OK. Now this is where the months of cross-referencing pay off,' said Marek. 'The first thing we do is find a copy of this photo in the sequential piles.' Walker followed him out of the office and into the studio where trays of pictures were stacked up against the walls. Marek pulled out a couple of trays until he found a copy of the photo. 'OK, so it was taken at about quarter to eleven. Good. Now we can try to guess where he's going and look at the relevant stuff—but if he doesn't crop up there we can resort to the sequential piles, look at every picture from eleven o'clock onwards.'

Marek moved along the rows of photos and pulled out four bulging trays. 'OK, he's walking towards Via Pisano. Let's assume he continues down there, so the next place to look for him is probably the Piazza Venezia.'

Marek's hunch was right. Within an hour they had found Malory again, blurred, recognizable only by his clothes, on the edge of a snap of a boy feeding pigeons. From there Marek reckoned he would have headed down towards Via Salavia. Finding no trace of him there they resorted to the sequentially arranged piles and found him, at 12.15, on the corner of two small streets.

So it went on and by mid-afternoon they had built up a stack of photographs. Walker was amazed how often he had strayed accidentally into the camera's gaze. The camera was a god, nothing escaped it.

They continued to track Malory's progress through the city. Marek pinned up a street map and marked out the route Malory had taken with approximate times. They came across him on the edge of a carefully composed shot of the Piazza San Pietro. After Repubblica this was the busiest and most intensely photographed spot in the city and two more photos followed his track from the northwest to the southeast of the piazza. Next he could be seen in the perfectly focused middle distance of a snap showing a hopelessly blurred young couple. This was followed by a sequence of video footage which, in the process of tracking across a piazza, showed him walking down an alley connecting Via Romana to Via del Corso—where he was duly picked up in the margins of a shot of a statue of Garibaldi framed by a heavily polarized sky. In a photo of a girl in a white dress, stooping down to examine the sandals and belts being sold by patient Africans, Malory was seen walking towards the edge of the frame. In Via San Marco he was snapped inadvertently stepping between the photographer and his intended subject. For a moment he could be glimpsed in a sequence of Super 8, shot on the move as the cameraman walked through a crowd of people.

Then he disappeared for almost an hour. When they picked up his trail again he was in a wide-angle shot of the cathedral steps.

'What time was it taken?' asked Walker.

'Early evening. Look at the shadows. It's one of the last photographs before the light went. Soon after it got dark there was an incredible thunderstorm.'

This was the last photo of Malory they found. Looking through the remaining photos took little time: only specialist or exceptionally careless photographers continued snapping into the fading light of evening. By nine o'clock there were only a few photos showing the cathedral illuminated by green spotlights or streets filled with the volcanic ghosts of red and yellow car lights.

Walker took copies of the photos and map. Back in his hotel he spread them out on the floor. He levered open a beer, took a swig from the bottle and poured it into a glass. He sat on the bed, drinking, staring at the pictures on the floor. Always his attention was drawn to the photo of Malory on the cathedral steps. Marek had blown up the portion showing Malory walking into a full-length 8×10. The fact that it was the last photo of Malory lent it an automatic fascination but there was something elusively familiar about it too. Walker glanced back at the other photos, rummaged through them until he came to the first picture of Malory he had seen, the one cabled through to him at Kingston. It showed just his head, looking off to the right. Placed next to each other the two pictures were strikingly similar. Blocking off everything but the head and shoulders of the cathedral snap, he saw that it was a mirror image of the original photo. Successive enlargements had rendered details as coloured smears in one and grey smudges in the other, but these background blurs coincided. Both pictures had been printed—one the right way, the other the wrong way— from the same negative.

Walker stared at the images, not attempting to fathom the consequences or meaning of this discovery. He picked up the Dictaphone and tossed it on to the pillow. Poured another beer and drank it carefully, noticing the taste of each sip, the way the cold glass felt in his hand, the beads of moisture on the bottle.

It had started raining. The blinds rattled in the breeze. On the writing desk was a phone that looked like it had never rung. He lay back on the bed and pressed the record button of the Dictaphone, heard its slow whirring. The faint murmur of traffic outside. The cathedral bells chiming damply through the rain. He tried not to think of anything, only the details of the room: bedspread, wallpaper, wire hangers in the empty wardrobe, sachets of coffee and sugar on the dresser.

He went into the bathroom where blue towels hung on a rail. He stood under the shower and got out only when the water began running cold. He dried himself and climbed between the cold, starched sheets. On the bedside table was a clock showing the time in thin green numbers, a lamp which he flicked off and on and off.

HE LEFT THE HOTEL EARLY AND, WITH THE AID OF THE MAP, BEGAN to duplicate Malory's route through the city, trying to pass through each place at the same time that Malory had done. As he did so he was conscious as never before of the number of people with cameras. In the course of the day he would be caught dozens of times in a tourist's photo.

He saw the things Malory had seen: a cloud idling through the sky, ice-cream sellers, children, couples in T-shirts and slacks, people reading. He saw a pair of sunglasses lying crushed in the road, the darting shadows of birds, cigarette butts in the grass around the ancient walls. He noticed everything and everything he saw was like a memory. Nothing surprised him. What he saw dissolved instantly into memory as if some intermediate stage in the process of cognition had been skipped. He kept thinking of ways to articulate and understand what was happening but knew from experience that it was better just to let it happen, to let everything fall into place as it had to, without his understanding.

The day moved on, morning led to afternoon. He saw the sun congregate in piazzas, grit lying between cobbles; he saw the cool darkness of rooms where lives were going on. He drank a coffee in a bar whose walls were lined with photos of local football heroes. He stared at the brown flecks of foam in his cup. Crystals of spilt sugar. A rind of lemon in a glass. The twisted butts of cigarettes in an ashtray. A crumpled serviette. On the table next to him was an empty cup with a print of lipstick on the rim. Was it possible, he wondered, to reconstruct the identity of the woman who had been drinking from just that smudge of pink? Her life, the way she spent her days, the things she had seen, the men she had loved?

When he came out of the bar the light was turning lemon, preparing to fade. He continued following Malory's route around the city, passing through a maze of narrow streets until he found himself in front of the cathedral. Clustered round the square, squat homes jostled for space, their needs dwarfed by the vastness of the cathedral's spatial claim. Walker looked up at the twin towers rearing above him, his eyes dragged skyward. The cathedral leapt upwards, every part of it straining to be higher than every other part. Graceful, full of grace.

The sun slipped behind the other buildings of the town, leaving only the twin towers of the cathedral in sunlight. Walker pushed open the wooden door and walked in. The cathedral was empty, no people and no pews. Walker made his way up the nave, his footsteps disturbing a silence distilled over five hundred years, accentuated by the clamour of vaulting overhead. The air smelt stagnant and fresh, reminding him of the chapel in the country. Flowers blowing by the old walls, brown earth. Purple and yellow petals, moving in the wind.

He looked up at the stained-glass windows where imploring figures blazed with colour: a knight in blue-white armour, a woman clutching a golden cup in both hands as if simultaneously praying and offering it to him. He walked past waving candle flames, the tombs of dead knights.

In front of the altar was a lectern and a heavy Bible. He opened the Bible at the page indicated by a dark ribbon and found an envelope there, crushed flat by the weight of pages, his name written in ink. The sound of ripping paper reverberated around the cathedral as he tugged open the envelope. Inside, folded in three, were the documents Rachel had given to him, signed and fingerprinted. He flicked through the papers and looked inside the packet again, searching for a note of explanation. Nothing.

The whine of hinges made him turn around. Three figures, Carver in the middle, were silhouetted as sunlight squeaked in through the open door. Walker moved into the shadows of the choir. The door swung shut. The three figures made their way towards him.

Walker knew nothing about the layout of a cathedral: if there were other doors he had no idea where they might be. Instead of a door he found himself by the steps leading up to one of the cathedral's twin towers. Glancing back at the figures moving methodically through the nave, he began climbing up the cold wide steps. The spiral of the stairs gradually tightened. He heard footsteps coming up behind him; he was being forced upwards, his options narrowing the higher he got.

As the footsteps drew closer he waited at a sharp twist in the stairs, his hand grasping the spine from which the stairs spiralled out. A man's head—Walker recognized him from the roof at Ascension—bobbed into sight. A second later his peering eyes looked up as Walker's foot smashed into his throat. He tumbled down the steps and Walker charged after him, catching him again full in the face as he scrambled to his knees. He grabbed Walker's ankle and they both crashed down more steps. He had ended up on top of Walker. His knees were pressing down on his chest, fingers digging into his throat. Shifting his weight, Walker succeeded in toppling him over and down the steps. Walker scrambled to his feet, clutched the rope handrail, and kicked at him again. The man covered his head and rolled further down the stairs so that it seemed they would go on and on like this with Walker dribbling him back to the floor of the cathedral. He lashed out at him again and this time he became wedged in the curve of the stairs and lay still.

He could hear more footsteps below. He stood for a moment, breathing heavily, unsure what to do, and then moved on up again. Blurs of purple and orange flashed before his eyes. He came to a small recess and a door which was locked shut by age. He kicked at it and the door tore loose from one of its hinges, the late sun blazing red through the gap. He kicked at the door again and it came completely free, a bird's nest smashing apart as it crashed open, two eggs dropping through the air and smashing on the narrow ledge. He stooped through the door, surrounded by red-tinged sky, his feet slithering in shattered egg. He was on a narrow ledge that ran around the tower. A bird squawked and lunged at his head: the flap of filthy wings, the eye-jabbing beak. He swiped the bird away, thought of trying to move out around the ledge but realized it was pointless—they would guess exactly where he was. He moved back in and ran up a few more steps before crouching silently in the twist of the stairs.

Seconds later he heard someone go into the recess from which he had just emerged. He tried to imagine the man's movements, pictured him looking at the sun-filled doorway, guessing that Walker had moved out on to the ledge but hesitating for one, two, three seconds before stepping out after him.

Walker, too, hesitated for crucial seconds and then stepped quietly down and back into the recess. There was no one there: he had moved out on to the ledge. Immediately, the figure appeared back in the doorway, black against the red sun. They saw each other at the same moment. Walker ran towards him. Crouching awkwardly, the silhouette braced himself and kicked out. A foot caught Walker on the side of the head but he shoved through the flailing arms and feet until they were both on the far side of the shattered door. He continued shoving at the figure who was pounding at him with one hand and grabbing on to the rusted hinge, trying to anchor himself, with the other. Walker wrenched a hand free and shoved him back towards the edge. He had lost his balance but was grabbing at Walker's lapels, dragging him as he stumbled out on to the ledge. They were both about to go over. Walker pushed once more, shrugged his shoulders and pulled back so that his jacket came over his shoulders and off. His assailant stumbled back, one step, two, clutching the jacket as if a flapping bird were attacking him. The next second there was nothing there except the sun's vacant redness.

Walker moved up again. His legs burned with the strain of running, air scorched his throat. The steps led eventually to a locked door that he couldn't budge. He moved back down until he came to a narrow paneless window. Leaning out he saw a ledge, just wide enough to enable him to move along to a decorative stone tendril running up to the roof of the tower.

Hearing footsteps below he squeezed through the vaulted window and on to the ledge. From here the whole city appeared to have congregated around the cathedral. In the distance the foil flatness of the river glinted orange-pink. Gazing down, the sky seemed to have been stitched into the fabric of the building, into the narrow windows and flying buttresses. Everything was vertical except the distant curve of the horizon. It was not just the fact of his being pursued: something inherent in the cathedral itself drove him upwards.

The ledge was barely wide enough for his feet but there were sufficient handholds above his head to enable him to steady himself and move along slowly. He felt the wind plucking his clothes. A storm was blowing in over the city. He shuffled further and felt the ledge crumbling beneath his foot. Taking as much of his weight as possible on his hands he tentatively moved his foot, but the ledge was too worn to support him. It was impossible to go any further. He began to move back the way he had come.

Still three feet from the window, he saw Carver. He had climbed halfway through the window. One arm was curled round the central pillar of the window, in the other he held a rusted crowbar. There was nothing Walker could do: in one direction Carver was barring his retreat, in the other the ledge was unable to support his weight.

Carver was speaking but the wind snatched away his words. Then Walker heard him say, 'So this is it. The choice is yours. Either you hand over the envelope—or I pick it out of whatever's left of you when you hit the floor.'

The sky was growing dark. Oil-spill clouds rolled over the city. 'So which is it to be?'

Every moment was like every other. Walker said nothing.

'I almost forgot,' Carver said. 'I've got something for you. You left it in the hotel.' He put down the crowbar and reached into his pocket. Tossed a silver chain towards Walker. It landed on the ledge, close to his feet, slithered out of sight.

When he looked up again Carver had picked up the crowbar. He leaned out further from the window and swiped at Walker, catching him on the elbow. Sparks of pain shot up his arm. He inched his way along the ledge, digging his fingers into the old stones. He stretched his right foot a few inches further and felt the ledge start to flake away. This was it: he could not go even an inch further. Carver swiped at him again, smashing the knuckles of his left hand. His fingers slid from the wall, numbed by the blow. Still anchored by his right hand, he swung out in a short arc, left foot slipping clear of the ledge. Now he was facing out from the wall, scrabbling to find a purchase for his left heel, waiting for the life to return to his hand. He glimpsed the remains of the egg, smeared over the toe of his shoe like a smashed body seen from high above.

Thunder rumbled over the houses beyond the river. An army of clouds moved across the sky.

Walker glanced across at the cathedral's twin tower, gargoyles jutting out from it. In the distance, a thin jerk of lightning. Carver swung at him again, missed. The swish of air had been almost enough to swat him from the wall. He saw Carver lean out still further, so far that he had to clutch the edge of the window with his hand to support himself, preparing to strike. The seconds grew enormous, vast as lifetimes. Carver was drawing back his arm. Walker looked out across to the other tower.

He bent his knees and sprang out, diving for the opposite tower. The sky gasped. Air rushed around him. He fell through the net of sky.

His hands clamped around a gargoyle, ripping muscles in both shoulders. The impact was so sudden his right hand slipped clear. Before he had time to reach up again and steady himself his left hand, swollen, unable to take the weight, slipped free and he was falling again—until the fingers of his right hand hooked around the teeth of the gargoyle: hanging by one arm from the mouth of a monster, stone teeth biting into his hand.

The first sigh of rain. He threw his other arm up over the ridged back of the gargoyle. As he did so the whole of its lower jaw gave way in his hand, embedding in his fingers for a second and then disappearing before that arm curled around the gargoyle's neck too. His shoulders were on fire but he was able to swing his legs up, locking them around the gargoyle's back so that he was embracing it, his face inches from the leer of its shattered mouth.

Thunder boomed. The sky was full of rain, the gargoyle was spitting water in his face. He hung there, regaining his strength. Then began pulling and twisting himself around and on top of the gargoyle, one knee crooked over its spine, the other swinging clear. Grabbing its ear and using it as a belay point he hauled himself up and around until he was straddling the gargoyle like a wounded man, slumped over a stone pony in the drenching rain.

He vomited into the darkness. Lightning lashed the city. He looked across at the other tower but could see no sign of Carver.

Using the wall for balance, he shifted his position and began to move his feet on to the back of the gargoyle. The effort made him giddy but once he had steadied himself he began pushing upwards, his back and arms flattened against the wall until he was standing upright. His feet wobbled and shook on the narrow spine as he turned half around, looking for handholds, for a way of pulling himself on to the roof of the tower. At full stretch he hooked his fingers around a ridge of stone, greasy with rain. He paused, waiting for the giddiness to fade. Blood rushed to his head, nausea was welling up in him again. When it had passed he hauled himself up, scrabbling with his feet until he found a foothold. Knowing he would never make it if he waited, he pushed with his legs and pulled with one arm, the fingers of the other groping blindly and then curling over the edge of the roof. Taking his weight with that hand he reached up with the other. Then, knowing that only one final exertion was needed, he hauled himself up until his shoulders were level with the roof.

He locked one arm over the low parapet and dragged himself up. Collapsed on to the roof.

Blood thundered in his head. Dark lightning. Rain jabbing him awake. His head was in a puddle of black water. He raised himself on one elbow, pain wincing through his shoulder. Dragged himself to a sitting position.

The puddles all around were silvered by lightning. When he looked up he saw Carver shivering towards him through the rain.

He watched Carver draw closer, so exhausted that even the reflex of fear barely worked, too weak and full of pain to move. He started to speak but his voice was drenched by thunder exploding all around. By the time the noise echoed away, even the impulse to speak had left him. He squinted up through the rain stinging his face. Carver loomed over him, raising the crowbar like an axe.

Walker stared up. Waiting for everything to be over with as the sky split in two around Carver. Lightning leapt down the crowbar, igniting the figure holding it. Flames licked his head and body. The moment held like a vast camera flash. Then he toppled forward in the darkness. The smell of burning, the blackened shape steaming in the rain.

Walker lay where he was, rain lashing his face, his eyes scarred with the image of Carver blasted by lightning, arm and crowbar raised triumphantly as if he had summoned the power that consumed him. Walker looked across at the cathedral's twin tower, ghastly through the rain.

Lightning shuddered over the city.

Thunder like a huge groan.

It was mid-morning, buildings were taking in their awnings of shadow. Walker's train did not leave for an hour and he made his way to the station, limping slightly. His body ached everywhere. His left arm was strapped across his chest but any sudden movement made his shoulder flinch with pain.

Blue sky fitted snugly over the city. Jutting above the cramped buildings he saw the twin towers of the cathedral. At a café he ordered an espresso and sat watching people pass by, wondering what he had learnt from the events of the last months. Maybe he would feel differently in the future but, for the moment, the more he thought about it the less sure he became. It had not made him sadder or wiser. All he could say for sure was that he had applied himself to something and could now head home and feel content for a while. Walk down to the beach and watch the ocean heaving in. Sleep in the same bed, see the same things day after day. Like someone coming to the end of a shift at a factory, he could go home and put his feet up. The longer the search had gone on the more he had hoped for some ultimate revelation—but such expectations already seemed ludicrous. The best you could hope for was to be free from the itch of restlessness, for a while at least. To put your feet up. For nothing to happen.

He took out the photo of Rachel, looked at it closely for several minutes and folded it away again. It looked like a picture from a dream, proving nothing, promising everything. He sat for a while longer, paid for his coffee and got up to leave, careful not to jar his arm.

He walked down Via Dante until he came to the river. A film of algae concealed the movement of the water, making the river look like a green sponge, thick enough to walk on. Halfway across the ornate bridge he picked up a stone and tossed it into the river. There was a slight plop and a tiny rip appeared in the green film. A few moments later the rip had vanished and the green sponge was intact again. His eyes followed the river curving into the distance. Shuttered houses, a few gulls.

On the other side of the bridge was a pay phone. He dialled Rachel's number but there was no answer. From a window nearby—he looked around but couldn't locate it exactly—he heard a phone ringing: someone else who wasn't there. He let the phone ring twice more and then hung up. Perhaps it was just as well: if he was dreaming he did not want to be woken up, not yet. He wanted to speak to her but had no idea what to say. Maybe in the course of the journey home he would know. Or perhaps not then, not until he saw her. Perhaps not even then. Home: the familiar shape the word formed in his mouth.

The phone he had heard earlier was still ringing but it seemed fainter now, as if whoever was calling had almost given up hope. Walker picked up the receiver again and called Marek, who answered immediately.

'Hi, it's Walker.'

'Walker. Shit! Where are you?'

'I'm in town. On my way to the station.'

'But, I mean, what happened to you? Where have you been? Where are you going?'

Smiling, Walker said, 'If I remember rightly, there's a painting by Cézanne called something like that.' He listened to Marek laughing into the phone.

'It's Gauguin actually.'

'Gauguin. OK. Anyway, how you doing?'

'Fine, but what about you? Where are you going?'

'Home. My train leaves in half an hour. I was calling to say good-bye—and good luck with the film.'

'What happened, though? You found Malory?'

'Not exactly.'

'What does that mean?'

'Well . . . Like I said, it means I'm heading home,' he said, glad of the chance to say the word again.

There was a pause and then Marek said, 'Hey, listen, we found some more film. Super 8.'

Walker looked back across the bridge: people flowing over it, carrying bags of shopping, holding hands, wearing sunglasses and hats, tourists with their cameras.

'Walker? You still there?'

'Yes. What does it show?'

'You don't want to see it?'

'No.'

'You want me to tell you what's on it?'

'Yes. Sorry. Go on.'

'I think it must have been taken the day after, or sometime later anyway.'

Out of the corner of his eye Walker saw a bird swoop down and glide low over the river.

'Go on,' he said.

'It shows him on Via Dante, near the river. He walks over the bridge and stops in the middle. On the other side he . . .'

Walker opened his hand and let the receiver drop. It jerked and dangled, moving slightly in the breeze.

Walker limped away but for a few steps he could hear Marek's voice, growing fainter by the word, explaining how he had walked from the phone and across Via San Marco, leaving the river behind. Glancing back just once before disappearing into the crowds on Via San Lorenzo.

Afterword

The Search was my second novel, published in Britain in 1993. The date is worth keeping in mind because, reading it again now, for the first time in twenty years, I realize that it is as clearly pre-digital as *The Long Goodbye*. Almost nothing that happens in the book makes sense in an era of cell phones, online bookings, digital cameras, and—most tellingly—search engines. Jeez, it's almost *quaint*. In one way the physical mechanics and choreography of detective work have been reduced by the investigator sitting at a desk, clicking a mouse, opening new windows; in another they have been expanded by his being able to make phone calls while pacing the street or driving (or, in the case of Al Pacino in *The Insider*, while wading in the breaking surf of a sea of troubles).

My other three novels—*The Colour of Memory*, *Paris Trance*, and *Jeff in Venice*, *Death in Varanasi*—form such a natural group that I tend to forget about *The Search*. It has a plot for starters, whereas the others involve groups of friends and the unfolding of romantic possibilities in entirely plotless if progressively more exotic locations: Brixton, Paris, Venice, Varanasi (which suggests that I might have come to the end of the road, not simply geographically and novelistically but alphabetically as well). *The Search* raises certain generic expectations which are then gradually subverted, but it starts with the same romantic situation as the others—meeting a woman at a party with all the hopes and promise attendant on that—before moving into another kind of territory (and progressively more exotic locations). And I see that it shares many preoccupations with not just my novels, but the other books too, the ones that aren't novels. All that time Walker spends thinking about giving up! I was wanting to call it a day back then, when I'd hardly even got going.

My Italian publisher called the book 'a metaphysical thriller' which sounded cool. That I was under the spell of an Italian writer, Italo Calvino, especially *Invisible Cities,* hardly needs spelling out (though I did spell it out, of course, by mentioning one of his cities, Leonia, in the text). Other books and works of art were much—perhaps too much—on my mind too: De Chirico and Hopper are here, obviously, along with the medieval romances I'd studied at college and a bunch of films I saw slightly later. The stranger reading *Tom Jones* on a train is none other than the allusively youthful author himself, making a Hitchcock-like cameo appearance. Walker borrows his name—and some of his wardrobe—from the Lee Marvin character in John Boorman's *Point Blank.* I was always struck by the way that although Marvin claims to have no doubts about why he's doing what he's doing—'I want my money'—this explanation sounds more and more mystifying (to him) every time he repeats it.

I also used up a lot of real—as opposed to cultural—capital in the book. The original idea, for a hard-boiled thriller unfolding in imaginary cities, came to me while holidaying in Italy with a girlfriend in 1988, in Siena, Pisa, and Urbino. It draws heavily on a road trip through the US and down into Mexico with Fiona Banner—to whom the book is dedicated—in 1990. I wrote it in 1991 in New Orleans and in the Bay Area, and revised it when I got back to Brixton later that year.

I've taken advantage of the book's belated publication in the US to make a number of small cuts to the original text.

G. D.
BROOKLYN
SEPTEMBER 2013

GEOFF DYER's books include *But Beautiful, Yoga For People Who Can't Be Bothered To Do It, Paris Trance, The Missing of the Somme, The Ongoing Moment, Out of Sheer Rage,* and *Jeff in Venice, Death in Varanasi.* His many awards include a Somerset Maugham Prize, the E. M. Forster Award from the American Academy of Arts and Letters, and, most recently, a 2012 National Book Critics Circle Award for the essay collection *Otherwise Known as the Human Condition.* His latest book, about life aboard a US aircraft carrier, is *Another Great Day at Sea.* His books have been translated into more than twenty languages. His website is geoffdyer.com.

Book design by McSweeney's. Composition by BookMobile Design & Digital Publisher Services, Minneapolis, Minnesota. Manufactured by Versa Press on acid-free, 30 percent post-consumer wastepaper.

Also Available from Graywolf Press

Winner of the 2011 National Book Critics Circle Award in Criticism

A *New York Times Book Review* Editors' Choice

A *New York Times* Top 10 Nonfiction Book of the Year

"This is what I find most remarkable about Dyer: his tone. Its simplicity, its classlessness, its accessibility and yet its erudition. . . . [Dyer's humor is] what separates him from Berger and Lawrence and Sontag: it's what makes these essays not just an education, but a joy."
—Zadie Smith, *Harper's Magazine*

Paperback / Ebook available

The debut novel from "possibly the best living writer in Britain"
(The Daily Telegraph)

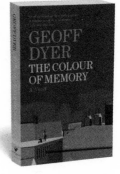

"Dyer writes crisp, Martin Amis-inflected prose, full of acute perceptions and neat phrases. . . . The book abounds in colourful descriptions of familiar aspects of London life."
—*Times Literary Supplement*

"Of all the hyped novels of 1980s London, it remains one of the most genuine."
—*New Statesman*

Paperback / Ebook available

WWW.GRAYWOLFPRESS.ORG

Many Graywolf authors are available to chat with your book club or classroom via phone and Skype. Email us at **wolves@graywolfpress.org** for further details.

Visit **graywolfpress.org** to sign up for our monthly newsletter and to check out our many regularly updated features, including our On Craft series, Pub Talk series, Poem of the Week, author interviews, special sales, book giveaways, tour listings, catalogs, and much more.

GRAYWOLF
PRESS

Graywolf Press is a leading independent publisher committed to the discovery and energetic publication of contemporary American and international literature. We champion outstanding writers at all stages of their careers to ensure that diverse voices can be heard in a crowded marketplace.

We believe books that nourish the individual spirit and enrich the broader culture must be supported by attentive editing, superior design, and creative promotion.